"You're making a terrible mistake!"

There was a long silence, her eyelashes fluttering nervously beneath his fierce gaze as he drew her tightly against his tall figure. She could feel his long, muscular thighs touching her own, and despite her very real fear of this dangerous man, it was some moments before her bewildered mind was able to recognize the nervous, quivering response feathering through her trembling body.

Oh, no! Surely, she couldn't be *sexually* attracted to this man . . . ?

MARY LYONS is happily married to an Essex farmer, has two children and lives in an old Victorian rectory. Life is peaceful—unlike her earlier years when she worked as a radio announcer, reviewed books and even ran for Parliament in a London dockland area. She still loves a little excitement and combines romance with action and suspense in her books whenever possible.

Books by Mary Lyons

HARLEQUIN PRESENTS

MARY LYONS

Love is the Key

Harlequin Books

TORONTO • NEW YORK • LONDON
AMSTERDAM • PARIS • SYDNEY • HAMBURG
STOCKHOLM • ATHENS • TOKYO • MILAN
MADRID • WARSAW • BUDAPEST • AUCKLAND

ISBN 0-373-11633-0

LOVE IS THE KEY

Copyright © 1992 by Mary Lyons.

CHAPTER ONE

How could she have been so foolish?

Sitting on a slatted pine bench amid the dense, steamy atmosphere of the dimly lit sauna, Tiffany glumly wiped the perspiration from her face.

If only she'd had the sense to check the date with some of her Portuguese friends, she would never have made the elementary mistake of arriving in Lisbon on the eve of a national holiday. Not that it was a total disaster, of course. But, having only a weekend to explore the old city before continuing her journey to England, she now had to face the fact that most of the important museums and palaces would be closed during Liberation Day—when the citizens of the country celebrated their release from a dictatorship which had ruled Portugal for many years.

To compound her mistake, she hadn't even bothered to book a hotel room. So, it probably served her right, Tiffany told herself gloomily, that all she'd been able to find, on her arrival late yesterday afternoon, had been a very small ground-floor room in a shabby hotel, tucked away in a side-street off one of the main avenues.

Since the whole city seemed to be preparing for the grand processions tomorrow, and with no conducted tours available, the opportunity to have a swim and a sauna in this glamorous health club next door to her hotel had proved to be irresistible.

However, despite looking forward to all the festivities tomorrow, she couldn't shake off her feelings of deep disappointment and depression. She had hoped that this trip would mark the beginning of a fresh new life, but it seemed to Tiffany as if she was still being hounded by forces beyond her control; the unhappy trials and tribulations which had dogged her life for the past few years.

Unfortunately, she couldn't blame anyone for her first serious error. By running away from home to marry Brian Harris she had, quite frankly, cooked her own goose. And when her hasty marriage had quickly disintegrated—as all her friends and relatives had accurately forecast that it would—she'd been far too proud to admit that she'd made a disastrous mistake.

'When it all goes wrong, don't bother to come running home,' the elder of her two aunts had told her sternly. 'Because, as far as we're concerned, you no longer exist!'

Tiffany had barely listened to the dire warning of her only relatives. Especially since it was her lonely 'existence' in her elderly aunts'. gloomy Victorian house in Eastbourne—where she had lived since the death of her parents in an air crash, when she was ten years of age—which had been the main impetus behind her decision to run away from home.

As always, when thinking of the death of her mother and father, Tiffany felt a pang of deep sadness. In the fourteen years since she'd been left an orphan, she had never ceased to mourn the loss of her parents' love and laughter—both so conspicuously absent from her aunts' austere, harshly controlled way of life. The boarding-school to which they sent her had been an equally unfriendly, ugly pile of Victorian architecture—but at least she'd been able to make some friends, although none of them had been welcome to visit her during the holidays. So, was it any wonder that she'd fallen madly and hopelessly in love with the very first glamorous man she'd ever met?

An emotionally starved eighteen-year-old, Tiffany had thought Brian Harris—a minor tennis star, who'd been making a promotional visit to her local town—to be the hero of all her young dreams. Far too young and innocent to see beneath the handsome tanned face and long mahogany legs, so graphically displayed beneath his whiter-than-white tennis shorts, she'd thrown all caution to the winds and followed Brian to London.

The only amazing fact of the whole miserable affair had been why Brian should have taken any notice of the star-struck, foolish young girl. Maybe he'd rather liked being idolised, and treated as though he were a divine being? Whatever the reason, it was now clear to Tiffany that her adoring, naked worship must have acted like soothing ointment to his bruised ego. Because, completely unbeknown to her, Brian's inability to resist the temptations of wine, women and song meant that he was already slipping down the ranks of the world tennis ratings.

However, wildly in love with the man of her dreams, she wouldn't listen to any good advice—not even from her schoolfriends, who were quite capable of seeing through Brian Harris's glamorous façade to the weak, shallow personality beneath.

And, of course, everyone had been quite right. Life on the American tennis circuit was very hard at the best of times—and there had been very little 'best times' about her marriage to Brian. With no permanent home, and always living out of suitcases in second-class hotels, which rapidly became third- and fourth-class hotels as his career continued to decline, their marriage had clearly never stood a chance.

Possibly, if she'd been older and more experienced, Tiffany might have been able to make a success of such a turbulent life. But it was, unfortunately, her total ignorance of sexual matters which had caused the first immediate rift, and from which their relationship had never recovered. Bored by her frightened rigidity and lack of response—and not even prepared to make any allowances for her youth and innocence—Brian had quickly grown tired of his new wife, returning to his old bachelor habits of swift sexual conquests with sophisticated women who, as he'd told her, 'knew how to enjoy a good time'.

How matters would have turned out, or whether Tiffany would have eventually found the strength of will necessary to leave her husband, she never knew.

Two years after their marriage—which was by now well into injury time—Brian had left her alone in a shabby hotel room in the Algarve, in Portugal, to go to a party given by some old friends of his. Deaf to her pleas that it wasn't a good idea—especially before a match due to be played the next day—Brian had been obviously drunk when, returning to the hotel late at night, he'd driven his hired car off the road. Contacted by a local hospital, Tiffany had learned that her husband was in a coma—and not expected to survive the night.

However, for almost a year, Brian had survived. Never regaining consciousness, he had remained a pale, silent figure in the hospital bed, whom Tiffany had visited as often as she could. It wasn't always possible, because the mounting hospital bills meant that she had to take any job she could find. Which meant working in local hotels and cafés to pay the medical expenses, and to keep a temporary roof over her own head.

With the memory of her aunts' last words still ringing in her ears, Tiffany had been far too proud to ask them for any financial help. And when Brian had eventually died without regaining consciousness, she'd barely had time to mourn the tragic loss of her young husband. With no other source of income, she was forced to keep on working, to save enough money for her eventual return to England, where she hoped to train for some form of career.

After a great deal of effort, she had managed to accumulate a small nest-egg. It was just about enough, if she was *very* careful, to enable her to exist for some months before she found a job. However, she hadn't been able to resist dipping into her small savings, and breaking her journey in Lisbon—a city she'd been longing to visit—before taking the plane on to London.

The loud, hissing crackle of cold water being tossed on to hot coals suddenly broke into Tiffany's thoughts. Raising her head and peering through the dense, heavy cloud of steam, she became aware of a shadowy female figure regarding her with a puzzled expression.

Tiffany was sure that she'd never seen the other person before, and yet there was definitely *something* familiar about the woman's face and figure. However, only later, when sitting in front of the mirror in the changing-room, did she discover the answer to her question.

'I always find saunas so *fearfully* exhausting—don't you?' a towel-robed figure drawled some moments later, as she sat down in an adjoining chair.

'Yes, they can be rather tiring,' Tiffany murmured, surprised and relieved to come across someone speaking English, especially as she only knew a few words of Portuguese. 'In fact, I . . .'

But, whatever it was she might have been going to say was instantly forgotten—driven totally from her mind as she raised her head to look at the other girl in the mirror. Like Tiffany, she too was wearing only a towel wrapped around her body with another short white towel swathed about her head.

Open-mouthed with astonishment, Tiffany could only stare bemusedly at the other person who, as far as she could see, might well have been her own twin sister. No wonder the other girl had seemed so familiar—it was virtually the same face she saw every day in her own mirror! The very same wide forehead over arched, fly-away eyebrows; the same clear, translucent blue eyes set in a heart-shaped face.

It was a moment or two before Tiffany realised that the stranger was also rigid with shock, and staring at her with an equally amazed expression. However, the other girl was clearly able to pull herself together faster than Tiffany, as she threw back her head and gave a peal of shrill laughter.

'My God—I simply *don't* believe it!'

'N-no—er—no, neither do I,' Tiffany muttered, shaking her head and closing her eyes for a minute. However, when she opened them again, she could see that there was no escaping the truth: she and this total stranger looked as alike as two peas in a pod!

'I guess the odds against this sort of thing happening must be about a million to one . . . ?' the other girl said slowly, pulling the towel from her head. 'But maybe you've got black hair—or you're a redhead . . . ?'

'No...' Tiffany murmured, still feeling stunned and not really able to believe the evidence of her own eyes as she, too, removed her towel.

'It's difficult to tell when our hair is so wet—but it looks as if yours is only a shade or two darker, and a bit longer than mine!' The girl gave another incredulous laugh. 'They say everyone has a double, somewhere in the world, but I *certainly* never expected to meet her—and in a Portuguese sauna, of all places!'

'No...I...I'm sorry, you must think me a complete fool,' Tiffany mumbled with a helpless shrug. 'I...I can't get over the amazing coincidence. It feels so extraordinarily weird to meet one's double, if you see what I mean...?' she added lamely.

The other girl gave a snort of wry laughter. 'I know *just* what you mean! After all, it's happening to me too—right?'

Tiffany nodded, and made a determined effort to pull herself together. It wasn't an easy task, since she and this stranger didn't just bear such a startling resemblance to one another—she was also considerably shaken to note that their voices sounded quite alike, as well. Although the other girl was obviously English, it seemed as if she also must have spent some time in the United States, since they both had a very slight American drawl overlying their basic British accent.

Quite frankly, this whole affair was beginning to feel definitely spooky! Unless, of course, she was going to wake up in a minute and find that it had all been a bizarre, unnatural dream...?

However, when the other girl put out a hand and suggested that they introduce themselves, there was nothing dreamlike or unearthly about the firm clasp of her long, slim fingers as she announced that she was Maxine dos Santos.

'I'm—er—Tiffany Harris,' she replied, almost sagging with relief at the discovery that their names were so dissimilar. It would have been just *too much* for them to have also shared the same name! Slowly beginning to recover from the shock, Tiffany began to think that she might be guilty of over-reacting to the admittedly strange situation.

There was, of course, no question about the fact that they *were* both remarkably like one another. However, watching in the mirror as Maxine began to comb her blonde hair, Tiffany gradually began to notice the differences between them. Leaving aside the colour of their hair, she could now see that Maxine's teeth were a little more pointed than her own; that the curve of her mouth when she smiled was a tighter, more controlled version of her own broad grin. And while it might be her imagination, of course, there did seem to be a hard, somewhat speculative gleam in Maxine's blue eyes, which were now regarding her so intently in the mirror.

'Well, Tiffany, I guess this is a once-in-a-lifetime experience, for us both!' Maxine gave another shrill, high-pitched laugh. 'If you're not in a tearing hurry, and since there's no one else in here,' she added, with a quick glance around the changing-room, 'Why don't you tell me something about yourself? Have you been in Portugal long, for instance? It sounds as though you've spent some time in America—but maybe you're now a resident in this country?'

'No, I'm really just here in Lisbon for a short visit,' Tiffany began hesitantly. However, the other girl appeared to be so interested and understanding that she found herself telling Maxine all about her past, and that she was now on her way back to England, where she hoped to start a new life.

'I don't blame you for giving your old aunts the heave-ho!' Maxine grinned. 'But surely you must have some other relatives in England? Or someone who's looking forward to seeing you again?'

However, when she'd learned that Tiffany had no other relatives at all, the other girl was very sympathetic. Explaining that she was also on her own in Portugal, staying in her husband's old family home in Sintra, Maxine urged Tiffany to come and spend the weekend with her.

'That's very kind of you, but I'm afraid that I've already booked into a nearby hotel,' Tiffany said, explaining how she'd been lucky to find even the small ground-floor room when the city seemed so full of visitors.

'Well, you'd better take good care of your passport. During the holiday, there's bound to be a lot of pickpockets on the streets,' Maxine warned her, nodding in approval when Tiffany replied that she'd left her passport, traveller's cheques and her plane ticket to England in the hotel safe.

A moment later, Maxine glanced up at a clock on the wall and gave a shriek of dismay. 'Heavens—I've got to go! I must make an important phone call, and then call at my bank. Since tomorrow is a bank holiday, there's no chance of it being open again until Monday,' she explained, hurriedly rising to her feet. 'Look, I don't know what you have in mind for the rest of the day—but why don't I come by your hotel, in a couple of hours' time, and we can go out for a drink and an evening meal?' she added, undoing her locker and quickly getting dressed.

'Yes—er—I'd like that,' Tiffany murmured politely, although she wasn't *entirely* sure that she wanted to spend too much time in Maxine's company.

The startling resemblance between them was having a slightly eerie, peculiar effect on her. Although Maxine had been very friendly, Tiffany instinctively felt that she had nothing in common with the older, far more sophisticated girl, who was apparently married to a Brazilian aristocrat—a man whom, it seemed, she actively disliked.

Very conscious of her own shortcomings during her brief marriage to Brian, and despite having travelled about the world on the tennis circuit, Tiffany had been shocked to hear the other girl's bald statement: that she'd only married her husband for his money.

'Actually, darling, I was in a bit of a hole at the time,' Maxine had drawled. 'So it seemed quite a good idea to marry one of the richest men in São Paulo. But it's all been a ghastly mistake,' and she'd shrugged her shoulders.

Tiffany, trying to disguise her discomfiture at what the other girl was saying, was even more shocked when Maxine revealed how she'd managed to trap her husband.

'I told him I was expecting his child—and he, poor fool, fell for the oldest trick in the book!' She gave a shrill laugh, brushing her blonde hair into a swirling cloud about her head. 'And since Zarco is stupid enough to believe in the sanctity of marriage—he's well and truly stuck, isn't he? So, we've come to an arrangement whereby he keeps me in the lap of luxury, and we hardly see anything of each other,' she added with another cruel, spiteful laugh.

It was obvious to Tiffany that this woman who so resembled her physically was not at all a nice person.

However, since she could hardly refuse to have a drink with her, she meekly agreed to meet Maxine some hours later, giving the other girl the name and address of her hotel.

Trying to overcome her natural distaste at the way Maxine had talked about her husband, Tiffany had almost made up her mind to find a convenient excuse to avoid the other girl. However, when she returned to her hotel after another swim in the heated pool, she rapidly changed her mind.

Her hotel bedroom had been *completely* ransacked!

Totally stunned at finding all her clothes piled in the middle of the floor, and covered with sticky blue paint, it wasn't until she heard the sounds of hysterical screams from the adjoining bedrooms that she realised she wasn't the only one to suffer such a misfortune.

It appeared that the hotel safe had also been broken into, and it wasn't long before Tiffany realised she was in deep, *deep* trouble. Not only had three ground-floor bedrooms been vandalised—but her passport, traveller's cheques and aeroplane ticket were missing from the safe!

Some of the other guests had also lost their travel documents, and the screams of rage and fury—not to mention a Spanish lady who immediately lapsed into raving hysterics—left Tiffany feeling mentally bruised and exhausted. It was at this point that Maxine had come to her rescue.

It was some moments before she recognised the girl standing in the hotel doorway. Why Maxine should be wearing a short black wig she had no idea, but she *did* know that she'd never been so relieved to see someone, in all her life.

'Thank God you've come!' Tiffany gasped, hurrying across the small foyer of the hotel to place a trembling hand on the other girl's arm. 'I didn't recognise you for a moment, but...'

Maxine grinned and patted the deep fringe of her false black hair. 'It was so peculiar, the two of us looking so alike,' she told Tiffany. 'So, I thought it might be easier if I changed my appearance. What on earth's going on?' she added, staring over at the noisy crowd of wildly gesticulating people by the reception desk.

'It's a total disaster,' Tiffany told her gloomily, sinking down in to a nearby chair, and burying her face in her hands.

'Oh, come on—it can't be that bad, surely?'

Tiffany shook her head disconsolately. 'It's worse!' she groaned. 'Not only has some sneak thief broken into three of the downstairs bedrooms—one of which was mine—but some of us have also been robbed of our passports and money. And that isn't all...' She brushed a distracted hand through her long gold hair. 'All my clothes have been vandalised. In fact, I've nothing but this tracksuit I'm wearing—and a small amount of money in my purse which, luckily, I had with me at the sauna.'

Tiffany didn't know what she would have done without Maxine's help. The other girl was simply marvellous, quickly appreciating the problems involved with the loss of her travel documents.

'You'll have to notify the police and the British Embassy too, of course. But there's no point in your hanging around here. You might as well come and sort out all your problems, in the comfort of my home,' she'd said firmly, leading the bewildered girl

out of the hotel towards a large chauffeur-driven car
which was waiting outside.

'But what about my underclothes and my make-up,
and——?'

'That's absolutely no problem,' Maxine assured
Tiffany as she helped her into the limousine. 'We can
come back and sort out everything after the weekend.
As far as clothes are concerned, you and I are just
about the same size, and I've got masses of things
which I've hardly worn,' she added persuasively,
giving Tiffany a warm, friendly smile as the vehicle
began moving off down the street.

'I really don't want to impose on you...'

'Believe me—it's definitely no imposition!' Maxine
laughed. 'I've been very lonely up at that old house
in Sintra, haven't I, Tony?' she asked the chauffeur.

'Yep—you sure have!' he replied, barely turning his
dark head surmounted by a grey cap, as he steered
the car through the busy streets.

Tiffany couldn't see much of the man who was
driving, but she was surprised to discover that he
clearly wasn't Portuguese. As far as she could tell, the
chauffeur came from somewhere not a million miles
from Brooklyn.

Seeing her surprise, Maxine gave one of her shrill
laughs. 'I wouldn't be without dear Tony for the
world! When I travel, he acts as my chauffeur and
general factotum. That's right, isn't it, Tony?' she
added with a giggle.

'You're the boss, lady!' he agreed in a nasal drawl.
'All the way to Sintra, huh?'

'You got it!' Maxine giggled again, the heavy
amusement in her voice and the slightly feverish,
sparkling glint in her blue eyes making Tiffany feel
rather uncomfortable.

Relax! Just be grateful for small mercies, she lectured herself sternly. Or large ones, in this case, she amended quickly, wondering what she would have done without Maxine's generous help. Settling back in the soft, luxurious leather seat, she tried to forget her worries as the vehicle left the city, speeding along the motorway towards Sintra.

The summer residence of the old Kings of Portugal, and of the Moorish rulers of Lisbon before them, Sintra seemed to be a magical place of romantic green, wooded ravines. As they approached the town, Tiffany's eyes widened at the sight of the ornate palaces and monasteries clinging to the sheer cliffs of the mountain range, with shady paths leading to wide green parks which, at this time of year, seemed to be filled with huge clumps of flowering camellias.

However, she hadn't realised that Sintra was so far away from the centre of Lisbon. When she mentioned as much to Maxine, her new friend pooh-poohed the idea that it might make difficulties in obtaining a new passport.

'With the public holiday tomorrow, which is a Friday, you haven't a hope of replacing all your documents until after the weekend,' Maxine assured her as the large limousine left the narrow streets of Sintra behind them. 'So, why don't we have a lazy weekend, possibly visiting one or two of the local sights, and then I'll get on the phone for you first thing on Monday morning?'

With a slight sigh, Tiffany realised that there was nothing she could do about the situation. And in fact, she reminded herself once again, she ought to be thanking her lucky stars that she'd been so fortunate to meet Maxine this morning.

When they arrived at the Quinta dos Santos, she could hardly believe her eyes. Maxine had referred to her house as a 'villa'—but she thought it looked more like a small palace!

'Hideous old pile!' Maxine grumbled as they got out of the car. And when Tiffany enthused about the pale faded apricot-coloured walls of the classical mansion, her new friend just shrugged her shoulders.

'Although my husband, Zarco, had a Brazilian father, his mother was Portuguese. This *Quinta* was her old family home, and when her husband died she returned to live here until her own death over five years ago. The house has been uninhabited ever since.' Maxine pulled a face as she opened the front door. 'So, I'd better warn you that it's a bit grim inside.'

'But it's fantastic!' Tiffany gasped as she stood in the centre of the hall, admiring an enormous tapestry, the colours of which seemed almost as bright today, as when it was woven many hundreds of years ago.

'Wait until you see the salon,' Maxine warned her, leading the way through wide double doors in to a much larger, if somewhat darker room. 'This place gives me the creeps,' she added over her shoulder as she went over to pull open the heavy, deep rich velvet curtains across the wide arched windows.

'Would you like me to remove the dust sheets from the furniture?' Tiffany asked, surprised that it hadn't already been done. 'That might help to make you feel more comfortable here.'

Maxine shrugged. 'I haven't bothered, mostly because I can't see anything making much difference to this dump. But removing those gloomy sheets might make it feel slightly more homely,' she agreed carelessly. 'Anyway, make yourself at home, and I'll fix us a drink in a few minutes. I've just got to put this away,' she added, indicating the large wicker basket which she'd been firmly clutching since they'd entered the house. 'I won't be a minute.'

Wandering idly around the room, Tiffany tried to understand the other girl's dislike of what was, for her, a truly lovely house. Everyone couldn't be expected to share the same tastes, and it was silly to feel disappointed at Maxine's jaundiced view of this charming room, she told herself firmly. By the time her new friend had rejoined her, Tiffany had swept away the sheeting from the elegant Portuguese furniture, and was idly studying a group of silver-framed photographs on a large table.

'I've made you a nice stiff gin and tonic—OK?' Maxine said, coming to a halt beside her with the two glasses in her hands. 'Oh, my God, just *look* at some of those old pictures—aren't they a hoot?' she said, handing Tiffany a drink.

'Some of the women's dresses do look a little old-fashioned,' Tiffany agreed. 'But who's this?' she asked, picking up a more recent photograph. 'I must say, he looks daunting!'

Maxine gave a shrill, caustic laugh. 'He does, doesn't he? And although they say the camera doesn't lie—I can assure you that Zarco is *far* worse in person! Yes,' she added as Tiffany turned to look at her in surprise, 'that's a picture of my *dear* husband. He must have given it to his old mother, just before she died.'

Having been thoroughly shocked by the other girl's cynical remarks about her peculiar-sounding marriage—how could anyone bring themselves to marry a man, just because he was extremely wealthy?—Tiffany didn't like to comment any further. But she couldn't prevent her eyes being drawn towards the strong, handsome features of the man in the photograph. It was almost uncanny, the way that the photographer had managed to capture such force and strength from his subject, and for the rest of the day those dark fiery eyes seemed to follow her whenever she was in the room.

Later that night, while drifting off to sleep in one of the villa's palatial bedrooms, Tiffany tried to make some sense of what was clearly a rather unusual household.

First of all, there was this really very large and beautiful house, which didn't seem to have any servants at all—other than the chauffeur, Tony, whom Maxine had rather vaguely intimated she'd brought with her from America. And there was no doubt of Tony's nationality. If anyone had asked her, Tiffany would have immediately said that he reminded her of some Mafia hoodlum. In fact, if it weren't too ridiculous, she could easily imagine him making her 'an offer she couldn't refuse'! However, since she'd had no experience of chauffeurs, she was hardly in a position to judge, she told herself sleepily. Whatever her reservations about Maxine herself, there was no doubt that without the other girl's timely rescue from the hotel in Lisbon goodness knows where she would have spent tonight. Certainly not in this supremely comfortable bed.

However, she felt distinctly ill when Maxine woke her the next morning, at the late hour of eleven o'clock.

'I feel *dreadful*!' Tiffany moaned, putting a trembling hand to her aching head, her mind feeling extraordinarily thick and sluggish, as if she'd been drugged, or had drunk too much. Which was ridiculous, of course, since she'd only had one glass of red wine at supper. However, it took her some time to focus her eyes on the other girl, who was placing a steaming cup of coffee down on the bedside table.

Although her brain felt as if it were stuffed full of cotton wool, she couldn't help wondering why Maxine was still wearing that hideous black wig. However, as her new friend pointed out, it might help to make them feel less strange with one another.

And she was quite right, Tiffany acknowledged some hours later. Although she was still feeling faintly muzzy in the head, she'd welcomed Maxine's suggestion that a breath of fresh air would do them both some good.

'I thought you might like to see Cabo da Roca before we go back to the villa. There's a lighthouse on the edge of the cliff, overlooking the sea, where you can buy a certificate to say that you've been to the "most Western point of Europe"!'

'That sounds fun.' Tiffany tore her eyes away from the passing scenery, watching as Maxine leaned forward to tap Tony on the shoulder—indicating that he should take the road lying between the vineyards of windswept sandy soil, rolling away towards the Atlantic Ocean. The awful wig, with its deep fringe hiding Maxine's wide brow, was very effective in removing the rather weird, uncanny feeling Tiffany had felt yesterday every time she'd gazed at the other girl's face.

It was yet another kind and thoughtful gesture on Maxine's part, she reminded herself—like the other girl's generous provision of one of her own dresses, and some costume jewellery, which Tiffany was wearing at this very minute.

Goodness knows, it was *years* since she'd worn a dress of this quality...not since her parents were alive.

Simply cut in a classic style, it was made from fine sapphire-blue silk which exactly matched her eyes. Relishing the feel of the soft material against her skin, Tiffany reminded herself once again of just how fortunate she was to have met Maxine. Even the elegant Ferragamo shoes fitted her feet to perfection. She knew that she wouldn't have been human if she hadn't revelled in the sheer luxury of such clothes, which she couldn't hope to be able to buy herself.

'Here we are—there's the lighthouse!' Maxine called out, her unnaturally tense, excited voice cutting into Tiffany's thoughts. 'Let's get out and take a walk along the cliff,' her new friend added as Tony brought the car to a halt.

'I'm...I'm not very good with heights, I'm afraid,' Tiffany muttered, shivering in the fresh sea breeze.

But it seemed her new friend was determined that she should view the sight of the ocean, pounding against the rocks many hundreds of feet below the cliff.

'Don't be so *stupid*!' Maxine exclaimed in a hard voice, her fingers tightening around Tiffany's slim arm as she practically dragged the girl's reluctant figure towards the edge of the cliff.

'Let me go!' Tiffany protested, suddenly gasping with fright as Tony materialised beside her, clasping hold of her other arm. 'What's going on? What are you doing?'

Tony gave an evil, spine-chilling laugh at her pathetic attempts to wriggle free of his hard grip. 'Don't worry, kid—I can guarantee you won't feel a thing!'

'Wait—*you fool*!' Maxine hissed urgently. 'We've got to change the wedding-rings—remember?'

But before her sluggish, drugged mind could even begin to understand what was happening to her,

Tiffany felt a sudden, heavy blow on the back of her head. And a brief fraction of a second later, she was falling...spinning down and down into an infinitely deep, dark void.

She was submerged—floating in a black swirling sea—living and breathing, but somehow protected from the world by a distant and hazy barrier of light and life.

A far-away light seemed to call to her, urging her up towards the surface of awareness. But as she became increasingly more buoyant there were many times when the encouraging light seemed to be blotted out by a dark presence. She had a strong sensation of menace and danger, which instinctively caused her to recoil, and once more sink back down into the comfortable darkness.

But eventually the light seemed to be pulling her through a long tunnel, and she rose up into a world of acute discomfort and pain.

The heat of the light seemed to be burning through her eyelids, which felt heavy as lead as she struggled to force them open. And yet, when she did so, her dazed and groggy vision saw that the space was illuminated by just one small lamp—the rest of the unfamiliar space hidden in shadowy darkness.

Trying to adjust her body into a more comfortable position, she gave a muffled groan at the sharp pain in her head, and she became aware not only of a throbbing, pounding ache in her brain—but that she was not alone in the dimly lit room.

'W-where...where am I? Who's there...?' she mumbled fearfully, suddenly feeling frightened and threatened by an unknown, alien presence. There was a long silence before she heard the sound of a heavy sigh, her dazed blue eyes widening as a tall, dark figure emerged from the shadows and walked slowly towards her.

The man stood looking down at the girl, whose hair was completely hidden by the thick bandage wound about her head. His body seemed immensely tall— huge and threatening as he towered over her supine, trembling figure. Her first overriding impressions in the faint light were of a barely leashed force; of tautly controlled anger in the tanned face staring so sternly down at her, the dark eyes glinting with unmistakable scorn and contempt.

'Who... who are you? W-what do you want...?' she whispered fearfully, her body trembling and her eyelids fluttering with terror in the face of such obvious malevolence.

'You know very well who I am. Who better?' he growled savagely, before giving an abrupt bark of cruel laughter. 'God knows what you've been up to, Maxine. However, after such a long and tiring journey from Brazil, I am decidedly *not* in the mood to play games!'

Another quick, fleeting glance at the stranger did little to reassure her—nor did it dispel the formidable sense of intimidation and oppressively strong physical threat embodied in his powerful frame. The dim light from the lamp threw deep shadows over his hard, arrogant expression, highlighting the few silver threads amid the midnight-black colour of his hair; the deeply hooded lids over those terrifying dark eyes emphasising the high cheekbones of his tanned face, and the cruel curve of his sensual lips.

'P-please...please go away!' she whispered, certain that she had never felt so frightened in all her life. The deep throbbing in her head seemed to reach an almost unbearable crescendo, and as she saw him raise a threatening hand something seemed to snap in her injured brain. A low, helpless moan issued from her lips as she lapsed back into the welcoming darkness.

The man froze, his brows drawn together in a deep frown as he stood motionless for a moment. And then he lowered his hand, to carry out his original intention of straightening the rumpled sheet over the slender, deathly still figure of the girl, who was now lying unconscious in the narrow hospital bed.

CHAPTER TWO

WHEN Tiffany next opened her eyes, it was to find herself staring up at a white ceiling, dazzled by its reflection of the bright sunlight flooding into the room.

Her brief groan as she tried to adjust her eyes to the glare provoked an immediate response. She was aware of a soft murmur, and of cool fingers being placed over the pulse in her wrist. As her eyes became slowly acclimatised to the daylight, she gazed uncomprehendingly about her. Dazed and disorientated, she knew she didn't recognise the bare walls of the room, or the stark blinds at the windows. And then a sharp pain as she tried to move her head obliterated any other desire to explore her surroundings.

A few moments later, her vision was filled by the sight of an unknown man's face looming over her. He appeared to be saying something and she strained to catch his words. But she couldn't understand him— not even when he began speaking slowly.

'What . . . ? Where . . . ?' Her lips felt rubbery, too dry and stiff to pronounce the words properly. 'Water . . . ? Please can I have a glass of water?' she whispered helplessly.

'*Inglês* . . . ? You speak English?' The man, whom she now saw was wearing a white coat, gave a slight shrug and turned to speak to someone outside the range of her vision. 'Very well, *senhora*. You want a drink of water, yes?' he asked, in a thick foreign accent.

'Yes . . . please,' she mumbled as, again speaking some incomprehensible language, he gestured to a white-clothed figure who materialised on the other side of the bed.

'But . . . but where am I? What is this place?' she gasped as a woman held out a glass towards her.

Trying to lift her head to place her lips on the edge of the glass, she groaned at the sharp pain which zig-zagged cruelly through her aching brain. The blackness seemed to be threatening to close in on her once again, swirling mists of agony blanking out the sound of the man's voice, until the painful sledge-hammer in her head began to quieten down into a dull, pounding throb.

'You are in hospital, *senhora*,' the man told her. 'And you must lie still. Not to move—do you understand?'

'Yes,' she whispered. With closed eyes she lay back on the soft pillows, trying to think why she should be in a hospital.

Some moments later she opened her eyes again, focusing with difficulty on the features of the man who was still standing beside the bed. 'Are you a doctor?' she asked, not finding anything familiar about the dark-haired, slightly sallow face which was now gazing down at her so intently. 'And, if this is a hospital— what am I doing here?'

'You do not understand anything about the accident?' he queried, again speaking English with a heavy accent which she did not recognise.

'No—I don't—er—I don't seem to be able to remember anything about an accident,' she murmured helplessly. 'And . . . and whereabouts *is* this hospital?'

'You are in Lisbon, of course.'

'*Lisbon*?' She winced as another agonising, jagged shaft of pain sliced through her head. 'Do you mean Lisbon—as in ... in Portugal?'

The doctor frowned down at the pale, heart-shaped face of the girl in the bed, whose head was swathed with bandages. He flicked his fingers at the nurse, who hurriedly handed him a chart from the end of the bed.

'Ah, yes. I see that you were brought in by the Guarda Nacional Republicana, three days ago.' And when she continued to stare up at him uncomprehendingly, he added, 'The police—you understand? They are wishing to see you about the accident, up at Sintra. And your husband, also. He has been most ...' The doctor paused, apparently hunting for a word from his limited English vocabulary. 'Most anxious ... yes, your husband has been most anxious to talk to you.'

'My husband?'

The doctor smiled down at her. 'Senhor Marquês dos Santos has been most worried about you. Many, many times he has been here, while you have been unconscious. So, he will be pleased to hear that you are awake, yes?'

Slowly she raised a trembling hand towards her bandaged head, which was now throbbing with painful intensity.

'I don't understand. I don't remember. Why am I here?' she moaned. 'I'm sure I'm not married—at least I don't think I am ...?'

'*Esteja quieta*! Be still, *senhora*. There is no need to worry. You have been very ill—but soon you will see your husband, and all will be well. But for now,' he added, before turning to the nurse and giving rapid instructions in Portuguese, 'I think it is time you had a good sleep. Do not worry. You will feel much better when you wake up.'

She would have protested further, but, following the sharp prick of a hypodermic needle in her arm, all protest seemed to die on her lips, and she once again drifted back into the warm, comforting darkness.

When she awoke again, she realised it must be evening, since the room was only lit by two pale lamps, and the windows seemed shrouded in darkness beyond their half-closed blinds.

It was the bustling presence of a young, dark-haired nurse which had brought her back to full consciousness, she realised, and was grateful for the girl's gentle care as she helped to raise her sore head, so that she could drink some water. But when the nurse said something in a language she didn't understand, she realised that it hadn't been a dream. She really was lying in a hospital in Portugal. Although how she came to be here, she still had no idea.

'I do not understand. *Je ne comprends pas*,' she added, in the vain hope that the nurse might understand her schoolgirl French. But it was clearly no use, as they both stared blankly at one another. 'I want to see the doctor,' she said as slowly and clearly as she could.

'*Médico*?' the nurse queried, and, when she nodded carefully in agreement, so as not to increase the background throbbing in her head, the other girl nodded and hurried from the room.

However, when the nurse returned, she was not accompanied by the doctor whom she'd seen earlier in the day, but by a taller, somewhat older man in uniform.

'I hear you've been asking for the doctor, Dona dos Santos,' he said in English, with a slight accent. 'But if you feel well enough, there are one or two important questions I would like to ask you.'

'Thank goodness you can speak English!' she murmured, almost sagging with the relief of at last being able to find out what had happened. 'I've been so confused. I mean, I've no idea why I'm here, in this hospital—or what I'm doing in Portugal, for that matter.' She gave him a weak, tremulous smile and raised a hand to her aching brow. 'I think there must be some mistake. Maybe they've got the names muddled up? Because I don't know why everyone keeps calling me "Dona dos Santos". That isn't my name.'

The man regarded her with his head on one side for a moment. 'Very well,' he said patiently, as if to a rather dim-witted child. 'What *is* your name?'

'My name is . . .' She frowned, staring down at the sheet for a moment. Why did her mind seem to be like a completely blank piece of paper? Telling herself not to be silly, and that it was important for her to concentrate on this minor problem, she tried again.

'This is so stupid, because of course my name is . . . My name is . . .' She raised frightened blue eyes towards the man standing beside the bed. 'I . . . *I can't remember*,' she whispered, a rising tide of panic beginning to flow through her body. *'I can't remember—anything!'*

'Don't worry, I'm sure everything will start coming back to you, very soon,' he said soothingly, as he opened a breast pocket of his uniform to extract a pad and pencil. 'Maybe you can recall what happened, up at Sintra?'

'No.'

'Or why you were there?'

'No—I told you, I don't seem to be able to remember *anything*!' she cried breathlessly, her whole body trembling with a numb sense of terror.

'Well—er—I will come back later,' he said hurriedly, looking up with relief as the door of the room opened and the doctor entered, followed a few moments later by a very tall, broad-shouldered man. There was a rapid conversation, in what she gathered must be Portuguese, between the doctor and the policeman, after which the white-coated doctor turned to stare frowningly down at her.

'I understand you do not remember? Not even your name . . . ?'

'No—no, I don't!' she cried fearfully, placing shaking fingers at the side of her aching temples. 'I just *know* that I'm not this "Dona dos Santos"— whoever she might be.'

'*She* happens to be my wife!'

She tried to turn her head towards the tall figure standing by the door—just on the periphery of her vision. And then, as he moved slowly across the room, she had her first clear sight of the menacing figure who had caused her to feel such terror last night.

Now that she was able to view him more clearly, the stranger's arrogant, tanned face and powerful body did nothing to dispel her first nightmarish impression of the man. There was still the same physical aura of spine-chilling menace about his tall figure, and she knew with an absolute and total certainty that she was not, and never had been, his wife.

Trying to shrink down beneath the covers, she gazed fearfully up at the man. His dark, heavy-lidded eyes were now empty of all expression as he viewed the girl's pale, frightened face beneath the heavy mound of bandages about her head; her slender figure now visibly shaking in the narrow hospital bed.

He seemed *so* tall! Although maybe it wasn't just his height and the width of his broad shoulders which made him appear to dwarf the other two men in the room. It was also something to do with the sheer force and power of his personality which, although he was still standing and regarding her in silence, seemed to radiate out to encompass them all. Even the policeman seemed to have shrunk a little, glancing deferentially at the man who appeared to so effortlessly dominate the room.

As her eyes flicked nervously over his hair, as dark as night and worn slightly long, curling over the pure silk collar of his immaculate white shirt, she found herself longing to be able to return to the peace and tranquillity of her unconscious state.

Everything about this man, from his obviously expensive, hand-tailored lightweight suit to the heavy gold cuff-links and the discreet glint of the diamonds on his equally heavy gold Rolex Oyster watch—clearly visible as he raised a tanned hand to check the time—appeared to shriek of wealth and privilege. What was such a man doing here in the hospital? He couldn't *seriously* be claiming that she was his wife...?

But it seemed that he was.

'Yes, this is indeed my wife.' The strange man's perfect English—clearly spoken for her benefit—sounded clipped and cool. Only a faint accent underlying the dark, rich tones of his voice betrayed his foreign origin.

The policeman turned towards her, raising a quizzical eyebrow. 'And do you, *senhora*, now wish to agree that this is your husband?'

'No...no, I don't!' she protested. 'I've never seen this man before in my life. Well, only very briefly, last night,' she added quickly. 'I can't possibly be married to someone and not know it, can I?' she begged the doctor tearfully. 'Especially not someone who's Portuguese——'

'Brazilian!' her so-called husband snapped irritably.

'But...but that's ridiculous!' she gasped. *'Brazil*? I know that I've never...I've never been to South America—and *certainly* not to Brazil. I mean...I don't even know what language they speak there or...or anything about the country,' she added lamely, flinching back against the pillows as the man who was claiming to be her husband threw her a scorching glance of contempt and dislike from beneath his heavy lids.

'I think it is time to call a halt to this farce!' he ground out angrily, before turning to the other two men. 'I can assure you that this *is* my wife. Unfortunately, while I do not know why she should deny the fact, I am sure that after I've had a few private words with her this simple matter can be sorted out,' he added dismissively with a shrug of his broad shoulders.

'Please help me!' she appealed to the doctor, helpless tears flooding her blue eyes as she realised that she was, somehow, trapped in what seemed to be a living nightmare.

'*Senhora...*'

'I really *don't* know this man!' she wailed. 'I've never seen him before in my life, and...and if I could only just remember my *own* name, I'd be able to prove it!' she cried, wincing at the pain in her head, and unable to prevent the weak tears from trickling down her soft cheeks.

'*Manten-te descansada...* Don't worry, *senhora...*'
the doctor murmured, before putting a hand on the
tall man's arm, and drawing him away from the bed
towards a corner of the room, where they were joined
by the policeman.

Almost drowning in misery, she was barely aware
of the low-voiced, rapid conversation between the
three men. It was only when the man they all regarded as her husband gave an exclamation of anger,
and was answered firmly and slowly by the doctor,
that she could make a guess as to what he'd been
saying.

The word 'amnesia' seemed to be the same in both
languages, although it took her a few moments to
understand just what the doctor meant. She must have
hurt her head at some stage, she realised, slowly
raising her hands to the crêpe bandages wound so
tightly about her head. Did she *really* have amnesia?
Could she have lost her memory? Was that why she
didn't know this terrifying man? But if so, why was
she totally certain that she wasn't married to him?

Her head was really aching with a vengeance, when
the doctor broke away and came over to the bed.

'It is very likely that the blow on your head has
given you what we call temporary amnesia,' he said,
speaking slowly so that she could understand what he
was saying. 'A patient with a head injury, such as
yours, can lose their memory for a short time. But it
will return,' he assured her earnestly.

'When? When will I get my memory back?'

He shrugged. 'That is difficult to say. Maybe soon—
maybe a few weeks. Maybe longer,' he added with a
frown. 'But yes, it will return.'

If it means being married to that awful, terrifying
man, I hope it *never* comes back! she thought hys-

terically, only just beginning to comprehend what was happening to her. And then she panicked, thrown into increasing terror and confusion as the tall Brazilian announced that he wished to be alone with his wife for a moment.

'Please...please don't leave me!' she whispered, feverishly clutching at the sleeve of the doctor's white coat.

'Ah, *senhora*, there is no need to be afraid,' he murmured, giving her hand a kindly pat, before gently removing her fingers. 'Your husband just wishes to have some words with you. I am sure he will be kind and... how do you say?... he will be understanding, yes?'

She very much doubted whether that man had *ever* been kind or understanding in his whole life! He certainly didn't hold those sentiments towards *her*! Despite being ashamed of feeling so weak and helpless, there was nothing she could do to prevent the tears from falling again as the doctor and the policeman left the room.

There was a long silence before the Brazilian walked slowly towards the bed. As she glanced fearfully up at the man looming over her, she was surprised when he merely shook his head, and handed her a large clean white handkerchief.

'I have to hand it to you, Maxine. I never realised what a consummate actress you were!' His rich dark voice was heavy with contempt, echoing the gleaming scorn in his dark eyes. 'However, kindly dry your tears, because I think this foolishness has gone far enough, don't you?'

'I'm *not* Maxine,' she protested, noisily blowing her nose before drawing on her pathetically small reserves of strength to add, 'and I *really* don't know you. I'm quite sure that we've never met—let alone been married to one another. And . . . and it's no good jabbering away at me in a foreign language, either,' she wailed as he swore violently under his breath. 'I simply don't know what you are talking about!'

He stood staring grimly down at the tearful girl for some moments, his face darkening with anger as he clearly strove to contain his temper. And then, when he once again had himself under control, he gave a heavy sigh and shrugged his shoulders.

'Very well, Maxine. You can continue this farce as long as you like,' he told her bitterly. 'However, I think you'll find that you are making a grave mistake. The police want to know what *really* happened out at Cabo da Roca? You were very lucky that a visitor to the lighthouse saw you struggling with a man and woman, and sounded the alarm before they could throw you over the cliff. And, incidentally,' he drawled with silky menace, 'I'd be interested to know exactly what you were doing there, too.'

'I don't know!' she moaned helplessly. 'I've never heard of this Cabo da Roca—and I've no idea what you're talking about!'

'Well, that's a matter for you and the police to sort out, isn't it?' The dangerous, threatening tone in his dark voice sent shivers of apprehension fluttering down her spine as she gazed helplessly back at him.

'However,' he continued, 'what does concern me is, why you are here in Portugal? As you know, we have an arrangement that you will remain at my house in England during term-time, while Carlos is at school. So, why have you broken our agreement?'

'I keep telling you . . . I don't know what you're talking about,' she moaned. 'And who is Carlos, anyway?'

'Please stop this ridiculous nonsense!' he hissed angrily. 'You may have fooled the doctor with this so-called amnesia—but you certainly haven't fooled *me*! Besides my religion, you know very well that the only reason we stayed married—a marriage which enables you to retain your enviable lifestyle—is solely because of the arrangement regarding my son, Carlos!'

She looked at him in bewilderment. 'A son? We have a child?'

'Do not try my patience too far!' he warned, his voice heavy with menace. 'And do not insult my son—nor the memory of his mother, my first and most beloved wife!'

'I didn't mean ... I didn't know ...' she whispered tearfully.

He gave a harsh snort of contemptuous laughter. 'All that is in the past—it is the present that now concerns us. You can rest assured that, even if the police fail to discover *exactly* what you were doing in Portugal, I most surely shall not! And when I do,' he purred dangerously, turning away with a scathing, scornful glance from beneath his heavy lids, 'I have a feeling that you will be very, *very* sorry indeed!'

And then he was gone, the room suddenly still and silent as the door clicked quietly shut behind his departing figure.

The next few days seemed to pass in a blur as she was subjected to exhaustive tests. Physically she appeared to be in reasonably good shape. As the doctor had pointed out, other than the wound at the back of her head, which had required a number of stitches, and the bruises on her face—which had apparently occurred when she'd fallen forward to the ground—she appeared to be in very good health. The stitches in her head had required the removal of some of her long hair. 'But it will grow again,' the doctor had told her with a reassuring smile.

'I . . . I don't even know what I look like,' she told him helplessly. 'I mean . . . I'm trapped inside this person—about whom I know absolutely nothing! I think I ought to take a look at myself, don't you?' she added with a weak smile.

'Why not? I do not see it can do any harm,' he agreed, before leaving the room and returning a few moments later with a small mirror, obviously the possession of one of the nurses.

Despite having wanted to see what she *really* looked like, she hesitated fearfully for a moment, taking a deep breath before raising the mirror. The first thing she saw was the large gauze bandage about her head, and then the faint bruising near her mouth and across her nose.

Almost instinctively, she raised a hand to a thick tendril of hair, the rich colour of old gold. Well, at least she did have *some* hair left, she told herself, even if, on further examination, it looked as if someone had attacked it with a pair of garden shears.

Staring at her face for a long time didn't seem to help. Was this really her? The pale, heart-shaped face with its high cheekbones and wide brow didn't seem particularly familiar. As she studied herself further, it appeared that her eyebrows were a slightly darker shade than her hair, arching in a graceful sweep towards her temples over wide, clear blue eyes with thick brown lashes. But she couldn't help noticing the anxious tremble in her full lower lip.

With a heavy sigh, she let the mirror fall from her hands on to the sheet. It was no good. She *really* had no memory of that face. In fact, it might well have been a stranger staring back at her with such fear and nervous tension.

However, while the doctor and his colleagues were not worried about her physical health, they did seem to be concerned about the state of her mind. When it became clear that she had no knowledge of Portuguese, she received a visit from an eminent psychoanalyst, who informed her that he was attending the hospital on behalf of her husband.

'I am informed by Senhor Marquês dos Santos that you should have a good working knowledge of the Portuguese language,' the gentleman informed her, settling himself comfortably down on a chair beside the bed. 'Although with a Brazilian accent, of course,' he added with a twinkling smile.

She had at first been determined to have nothing to do with this man, especially since he'd been engaged by her so-called husband. But the kindly light in his eyes and the sympathetic, concerned way in which he treated the problem, softened her attitude towards him.

'I don't know any way to prove I *don't* know how to speak your language,' she told him with a helpless shrug. 'In fact, although nobody seems to believe me, I don't know anything about this woman "Maxine". All I *do* know is that I feel quite certain that's not my name. And...and if I'd been called that all my life—surely that's the one thing which *would* be familiar?' she added with a puzzled frown.

'Not necessarily, no. It is quite possible for someone to completely forget who she is, and all trace of her past life,' he told her, taking a large pad of paper from his briefcase. 'Do you mind if I make some notes?'

'Go ahead. Everyone else in this hospital seems to be having a field day, at my expense!' she told him bitterly.

Calmly disregarding her outburst, he merely gave her another sympathetic smile and made a note on the pad.

'Who am I?' she demanded with impatience. 'There's this terrifying man—who, incidentally, doesn't seem to like me one little bit!—insisting that I'm his wife. But if so, I don't know anything about her. I don't even know how old she—er—I am supposed to be,' she sighed heavily. 'You see the problem—it's all a complete blank!'

He hesitated for a moment. 'I do not know about your intimate married life, of course,' he informed her quietly, lifting another file from his briefcase. 'But I understand from your husband that you are twenty-seven years of age...'

'That old?'

'...and that you were born in England, where you lived for most of your young life before leaving home, and going to live in New York.'

'New York?' she frowned. 'What was I doing there?'

He consulted his notes again. 'It appears that you were a fashion model for some time before you married.'

She lay back on the pillows for a moment, considering the information she'd been given. 'It all sounds very unlikely to me,' she said at last. 'New York doesn't sound too strange—but I don't *feel* as if I've ever been a fashion model. Are you quite sure about all this?'

'Oh, yes. Your husband has even provided me with a birth certificate,' he assured her.

'And I married my husband in New York?' she asked, gradually becoming interested in the life of this strange woman, of whom she had absolutely no recollection.

He shook his head. 'No, *senhora*. Your first husband died, and it was then that you went to live temporarily with your father and stepmother in São Paulo, in Brazil,' he told her, adding that her father had been the manager of a large, prestigious English bank in Brazil. Now retired, he and his wife lived in Rio de Janeiro.

'And that's where I met my husband—in São Paulo?' she asked, and when he nodded she could only respond with a slow shake of her head. 'I don't even know what my husband does for a living. And why haven't I heard from my parents?'

'Your husband is a very—er—a very wealthy businessman,' he informed her. 'I understand that, due to the current financial situation in Brazil, he is transferring many of his assets over here, to Portugal. He has told me that he wishes to spend more time in this country, principally to modernise his very large estates in the Alentejo, which is a large province in the south of this country. As for your parents . . .' He paused. 'I believe that there has been some trouble in the past, with your stepmother. Maybe that is why. . . ?' He didn't finish the sentence, but merely shrugged his shoulders.

'I don't think that I sound very nice,' she told him gloomily. 'Neither my husband nor my stepmother seems to like me very much.' She gave another heavy sigh. 'My husband mentioned his son, Carlos—but he's not *my* child, right?'

'Quite right. The boy, who is ten years of age, is the son of the Senhor Marquês's first wife, who died when the child was very young. He is at present in a boarding-school, in England.'

'Oh, the poor thing!' she exclaimed, suddenly having a fleeting vision of herself, clothed in a brand-new grey uniform far too large for her small skinny figure, sitting disconsolately by a classroom window as she watched the other girls being collected by their parents.

'I was always so lonely and...' Her voice trailed away as the brief vision faded, leaving her mind blank and void.

'*Senhora*...?' he probed gently as she stared blindly at him, her wide blue eyes filling with tears of frustration.

'I had a mental picture of myself at school—but it's gone! I can't seem to... I can't pull it back, if you see what I mean?' she told him in distress.

He nodded with understanding. 'It is quite normal,' he assured her. 'You'll have many more such "pictures" as your memory begins to return. But it is better if you do not try too hard. You must give your mind a chance to heal.'

When the psychoanalyst had gone, she tried to follow his advice. But she couldn't help striving to recall something—anything!—which would help to bring her closer to the mysterious woman, with whom she felt absolutely no affinity whatsoever.

Subsequent visits from both the doctor and the police officer, while not achieving any improvement in her memory, did at least provide some answers to the baffling question of how she came to be in hospital.

From the police officer she discovered that there was no question about her identity—certainly not as far as they were concerned. The man who had seen her struggling with two strangers, on the edge of the dangerous cliff overlooking the Atlantic Ocean, had fortunately disturbed the man and woman. They had left her lying on the ground, racing back to their car before driving swiftly away. And it seemed that they were still at large.

However, when the police and ambulance had arrived, her identity had been quickly established. The purse lying beside her body had contained not only her passport, but also her diary, charge cards and her first-class return plane ticket to London. And, if the police had needed any further identification, her husband had provided certain proof of her identity. He'd confirmed her appearance, and that the purse, her clothes, jewellery, *and* her wedding-ring, were all items belonging to his lawfully wedded wife.

So, it had rapidly become clear that no one had any doubts about her identity. As the policeman had pointed out: if she was *not* the wife of the Senhor Marquês Zarco dos Santos, who was she? And why had she been in possession of the other woman's belongings?

Her husband, on the other hand, clearly believed that, for some nefarious reason of her own, she was pretending to have lost her memory. And it wasn't until after another visit from the eminent psychoanalyst that Zarco—*very* reluctantly—began to accept the fact that she might not remember who she was.

'I suppose I *must* believe what the man says,' he told her grimly on one of his few, infrequent visits to the hospital. 'However, I know you, Maxine! Unlike the other credible fools in this place, I *know* that you are perfectly capable of pulling the wool over everyone's eyes. My only problem lies in wondering why. What you can possibly hope to gain?'

She *really* disliked this aristocratic arrogant man, to whom all the hospital appeared to be bowing and scraping whenever he deigned to visit her. In fact, if she really *was* Maxine—she couldn't think why she hadn't run away from the awful man, years ago! Every time he came anywhere near her, she found herself becoming suddenly breathless and sick with apprehension.

Even now, as she gazed at his tall figure in the formal suit, which seemed to emphasise the breadth of his shoulders, he was making her feel nervous. But she couldn't seem to tear her eyes away from the hard, firm line of his sensual lips, or the frosty glare from beneath the heavy eyelids—so sharply at variance with his cool, urbane stance as he lounged carelessly against the window-sill.

'Do you mean to say that the great Senhor Marquês Zarco dos Santos can't find an answer to such a small problem?' she retorted spitefully.

'Don't be impertinent!' he snapped, the only sign that she had managed to dent his iron control being the sight of a small muscle beating rapidly in his jaw.

'If you so obviously dislike your wife, why haven't you divorced?' she asked, still reluctant to accept that she could be a woman who, as far as she could see, was just about as nasty as Zarco himself.

'Because I have always taken my marriage vows seriously. *And* there is the fact that you have always refused to dissolve our union,' he ground out through clenched teeth. 'Also, as you well know, I have needed a mother-figure for my son, Carlos. Not that you have ever taken any interest in the boy, of course,' he added bitterly.

'Well, since you obviously wish that I was dead, maybe it was *you* who organised my "accident"...?'

she murmured, leaning wearily back on the pillows and closing her eyes. Life in a hospital was incredibly exhausting, and it seemed a very long day already, although Zarco had only been in her room for a few minutes.

'*Me* . . . ?'

She opened her eyes. 'Why not?' she muttered, gazing dully at the blank astonishment on his tanned, aristocratic face. 'From all you say, it would appear to be the perfect answer. Surely it would be easy, for a man of your wealth, to hire some thugs to push me off the cliff?'

'I would *never* do such a thing! It would be a mortal sin,' he retorted sternly, before pacing up and down the room. 'My code as a nobleman, and the pride I bear in my name—as a descendant of João Gonçalves Zarco, who with Henry the Navigator rediscovered Madeira in 1420—would forbid even the *thought* of such behaviour!' he added with resounding force and emphasis as he spun around to face her, his dark eyes flashing with rage.

Quailing beneath the onslaught of his fury, she dearly wished that she had never mentioned the subject. And as he advanced closer to her trembling figure, trapped in the narrow hospital bed, the raw force of his personality seemed to overwhelm her.

'Go away! Leave me alone!'

Her husky whisper seemed to hover in the air between them, her knuckles whitening with tension as she gripped the thin hospital sheet covering her trembling figure.

Zarco gave a harsh, sardonic laugh.

'"Leave me alone"' . . . ?' he mocked savagely. 'Have you really forgotten all those nights, when you tried to tempt me into your bed? The countless times you have endeavoured to entice me with the undoubted allure of your body?'

'*No*! That wasn't *me*!'

'And all to no avail!' he told her, ignoring her breathless denial as he leaned forward and whipped the sheet away from beneath her clenched hands. As she hastily tried to grab it back, their hands became entangled, his fingers becoming caught in the loose neck of her white hospital gown. There was a screeching sound as the thin, much laundered threads of the material gave way beneath the force of his action, and the garment was split open to her waist.

There was a long, stunned silence as she stared down in shocked disbelief at the display of her naked breasts. Numb with horror, she was unaware of Zaroo's hooded eyes devouring the sheen of her pale body, the sight of her full breasts rising erotically between the torn fragments of thin cotton.

'Yes, you have a beautiful body. But it is not one that I have ever cared to possess. Not since I discovered how you trapped me into our mockery of a marriage,' he snarled, ignoring her frightened gasps of fear and panic.

Since she was desperately struggling to pull up the tattered fragments of the gown to cover herself, it was some moments before she became aware that it was a hopeless task. Colour flooded her pale cheeks, strangled moans breaking from her throat at the realisation there was nothing she could do; nothing to prevent the continued exposure of her naked breasts.

'Poor Maxine...!' he murmured sardonically, contemptuously brushing the long tanned fingers over her nipples, the rosy tips involuntarily swelling and hardening beneath his scornful touch. 'How you have ached for my caress...yes?'

'*No!*' she gasped helplessly, unable to control the sharp, quick-fire excitement surging through her trembling body at his intimate touch, the breath catching in her throat as she fought against his deliberate and remorseless arousal of her emotions.

'You may lie—but your body tells me the truth!' he pointed out softly, looking down at her with cold, merciless dark eyes.

She swallowed hard, helplessly praying for enough strength of will to prevent her body from reacting with sensual delight to his blatant arousal. 'Please...please, don't do this to me!' she begged huskily.

'There's no need to look so stricken,' he murmured sardonically, before swiftly pulling up the sheet to cover her nakedness. 'I was merely demonstrating that I am not to be influenced by your feminine wiles. That even now I have agents scouring the streets of Lisbon, tracking down your movements from the moment you first landed at the airport, two weeks ago.'

She shivered uncontrollably at the hard, spine-chilling menace in his voice.

'And when I *do* find out the truth behind your "accident"—as I most surely will,' he added grimly as he turned to leave the room, 'I have a feeling that you would be well advised to start saying your prayers!'

'But...but what am I going to do about my gown?' she wailed, her cheeks flushing scarlet with embarrassment at the thought of trying to explain how the garment came to be torn.

He gave a cruel laugh. 'I'm afraid that, my dear Maxine, is a problem you'll have to solve on your own!'

The sneering contempt in his voice seemed to echo around the small room long after he was gone.

Sagging back against the pillows, she trembled with exhaustion, not only from the shock of Zarco's insulting words and behaviour, but also from her own reaction. How *could* her body have responded with such breathless excitement to the degrading, offensive way in which he'd deliberately aroused her? A deep tide of crimson flooded her cheeks once more as she recalled the aching pleasure engendered by the touch of his fingers on her breasts.

She was sure that never before had she ever felt quite so demeaned and humiliated, while the realisation that she appeared to be married to a man who regarded her in such a loathsome, scornful light was almost more than she could bear.

CHAPTER THREE

MERCIFULLY, it was some days before Zarco came to visit her again. And during those lonely, unhappy hours Tiffany's low spirits were suddenly lifted by the completely unexpected appearance of Mrs Emily Pargeter.

An aged relic of the old British Raj, Mrs Pargeter was clearly one of those indomitable women who believed in 'doing good' to her fellow human beings—whether they wanted such aid or not.

'Hello, dear. The doctors tell me that you are just the tiniest bit lonely, and don't seem to have any visitors,' the elderly, grey-haired old lady said as she bustled into the room one afternoon. 'So, I've come to cheer you up!' she announced, throwing open the blinds, and letting the brilliant sunlight flood into the room.

'We can't have you lying here in doom and gloom, can we?' she continued brightly, coming over to sit down on the bed. 'Now, dear, what is your name?'

'I've no idea. *They* say that it's Maxine dos Santos,' she told the elderly woman, who was regarding her with bright, inquisitive eyes.

'And who do *you* think you are, dear?'

'I haven't a clue! That's the trouble, you see. I don't *feel* as though I know this person, Maxine, at all. And quite apart from anything else,' she added, her voice rising in a mixture of fear and overwhelming exasperation, 'I think she sounds *horrible*! Her husband obviously hates her and . . . and even her own father and stepmother don't want to have anything to do with her!' she added, helpless tears of misery welling up in her blue eyes.

The older woman clicked her teeth sympathetically. 'Now come on, dear, have a good blow,' she said, handing the girl a handkerchief. 'There's no need to get in to such a tiff about something like this, is there? We must just try and see if we can't...'

'*What* did you say?'

Emily Pargeter looked at the young girl in surprise. 'I was just saying that you really ought not to get in such a tiff about——'

'Tiff... Tiff...?' She squeezed her eyes shut, desperately trying to catch the stray, brief thread of remembered sound which had suddenly illuminated the darkness in her mind.

'Well, of course I know it's a bit of an old-fashioned expression!' The elderly woman gave a laugh, which sounded like a horse neighing. 'My dear late husband, Brian, often used to tell me off for using slang words, like "tiff". Brian always said that——' She stopped abruptly as the young girl gave a strangled cry—and promptly burst into tears.

'Now really, dear! I can't believe that anything I've said could upset you like this?'

'No... no, you don't understand!' she sobbed. 'It was your words that triggered it off; I could suddenly hear and see my aunt Doris giving me one of her usual lectures. They always used to begin: "Really, Tiffany!" She and my Aunt Beatrice were always simply horrid to me, and——'

'Now do calm down, dear!'

'But don't you *see*? I've remembered something—at last!' She tried to smile through the tears streaming down her face. 'My name is Tiffany...Tiffany Harris.

And I'm married to Brian Harris—or I think I am...'
she added hesitantly. 'I keep seeing pictures of tennis
courts; always having to pack suitcases and staying in
hotels all over the world...' Her voice died away as
she lay exhausted back against the pillows.

'You've *no* idea—it's all such a relief!' she continued breathlessly. 'I mean...everyone, but *everyone*
has been telling me that I'm this awful woman,
Maxine. But I knew that I wasn't...I just *knew* it!
I'm quite certain that my name is Tiffany—and I
ought to know that, oughtn't I?' she begged, desperately catching hold of the other woman's elderly,
gnarled hand.

'Well, I think you're probably right, dear,' Emily
agreed soothingly. 'Now, dry these tears, and then you
can tell me all about the problem.'

Haltingly at first, and often breaking down into
fresh sobs of relief and exhaustion, Tiffany explained
what she knew of the events leading to her being in
the hospital. It was also a great relief to be able to
tell someone, especially another female, about her
shock in discovering that she was apparently married
to a Brazilian aristocrat, the Marquês Zarco dos
Santos.

'Goodness—how exciting!' Emily exclaimed.

'No, it's not! You've no idea how *awful* Zarco is!'
she told the elder woman. 'For one thing, he obviously hates his wife! And when I say *hate*—I promise
you that I'm definitely not putting it too strongly!'
she added with a shudder. 'Apparently his wife, the
woman he calls Maxine, shouldn't have been here in
Portugal in the first place—which is one of the things
he seems to be so cross about. And, just to make
things *really* complicated, while Zarco is totally convinced that I'm his real wife, *he* seems to believe that

I'm just pretending to have lost my memory!' she gulped. 'So . . . I seem to be caught up in the middle of a *very* complicated situation.'

'You poor girl!' the old lady murmured sympathetically. 'What are you going to do now?'

'I don't know . . .' Tiffany told her, her initial euphoria at the total certainty of her own real name draining away as she realised the problems that beset her. 'Everyone—except my beastly husband—is agreed that I'm suffering from amnesia. And, until I can *prove* that I am not Maxine, I don't see what I can do. But *you* believe me, don't you?' she begged the other woman.

'Certainly I do, Tiffany,' Emily Pargeter told her staunchly, but added with a frown, 'I do think you have a bit of a problem. From what you said earlier, it seems that you were found with a passport and documents all in the name of this other woman, Maxine dos Santos.'

'Yes, that's the trouble. I haven't got a shred of evidence that I'm really Tiffany Harris.' She lapsed into a gloomy silence. 'If only I could somehow get hold of my aunts,' she said at last. 'I know they were terribly angry when I married Brian—although I can't remember why. However, I'm sure they'd be able to back up what I say. But I can't do anything about it. Not while I'm stuck here in this hospital.'

'There is such a thing as a telephone, you know!' Emily told her with a grin. 'If you can remember your aunts' surname and their address—or better still their phone number—I can contact them for you, if you like.'

'Would you? Would you *really* do that for me?' Tiffany gasped, almost overcome with excitement at the thought of being rescued from the terrible situation in which she found herself. 'I'd be so grateful!'

However, she had to concentrate for a long time, lying back on the pillows with her eyes tightly closed, before she was able to recollect her aunts' surname, and their address in Eastbourne.

'I think that's right,' she told the old lady, who was busy writing the details in a small notebook. 'But I simply can't remember their telephone number, I'm afraid.'

'Don't worry, dear. I'm sure I will be able to get in contact with them,' Emily said, reassuringly patting the girl's hand. 'Now, I really must go. Keep your courage up, and I'll be back to see you tomorrow,' she added, before bustling from the room.

Despite all her excitement at having remembered her name, and the fact that Emily Pargeter was going to help to prove her identity, Tiffany found that she was extraordinarily tired and exhausted after the departure of her visitor.

Thinking about her talk with Emily, she realised that maybe she hadn't communicated forcibly enough *just* how formidable and menacing Zarco really was. How could she stand up to such a man? Especially someone so much older and obviously more experienced than herself. Not that he was really all that old, of course, she thought sleepily. It must be his ruthlessly arrogant, overpowering presence which made him appear so daunting...

Obviously far more tired than she'd realised, Tiffany slept heavily, not waking up until the next morning, when she found herself feeling immeasurably refreshed. Despite being slightly shaky on her legs, it was a relief to be able to leave her bed for the first time, and sit in a chair by the open window, savouring the bright sunshine and fresh spring breeze.

On waking up, Tiffany had been determined to assert her own real identity, refusing to be addressed by anything other than her own name. And, after some initial surprise and scepticism, the hospital staff agreed to her request, although she knew that they were merely humouring her—just as they might a spoilt, difficult child. All the same, it was one battle won...even if it was beginning to look as though she'd lost another.

As promised, Emily Pargeter had called to visit her, earlier that afternoon. But, after one quick glance at the older woman's face, Tiffany had known that she was the bearer of bad news.

'I'm sorry, dear. I did manage to obtain the telephone number, but, although the lady I spoke to confirmed that she *was* Miss Doris Kendall—she denied the fact that she had a niece called Tiffany.' Emily had looked at her with concern. 'The lady was very firm—almost unpleasant, in fact, I'm afraid.'

'Yes, she would be,' Tiffany had muttered with a heavy sigh. 'It's difficult to explain—but I can't remember things like phone numbers or the six-times-table. It's more . . . well, it's like seeing pictures in my head,' she had striven to explain. 'For instance, earlier today, I could *see* my aunt, absolutely furious with me for marrying Brian. I think he was a professional tennis player, although I'm not entirely sure.' She had shrugged unhappily. 'Anyway, my aunt kept saying, "We wash our hands of you! As far as we're concerned, you don't exist any more!" I can remember that she also said it was no good me running home, if my marriage ended in disaster—because they wouldn't want to know me any more.'

Emily had been very sympathetic. She had pointed out that it was only a minor set-back. It wouldn't be long before Tiffany was sure to remember more about her past life, and also the names of some friends who could substantiate her true identity.

Unfortunately, despite trying desperately hard, Tiffany's mind had obstinately refused to recall anything else. Maybe she was trying too hard? However, she found herself becoming increasingly nervous as she wondered how she was going to explain matters to her so-called husband.

With her aunts' denial of her existence, Zarco wasn't going to take a blind bit of notice of her, was he? Not when there was so much evidence stacked up against her. She hadn't just been wearing Maxine's clothes and jewellery—there was the matter of her passport as well. Above all, how could anyone—especially a hard, tough, confident man like Zarco—make such a mistake in identifying his own wife?

Going over these questions in her tired mind produced no answer—or not one that made any sense—and she was in a considerable state of nerves, when Zarco appeared unexpectedly in her hospital room that evening.

It was immediately apparent from the taut, tightly controlled expression on his face and the glinting sparks of rage in his dark eyes that he was almost beside himself with fury.

'Well, my dear wife—I now know *exactly* what you were doing here, in Lisbon!' he grated angrily, his tall figure looming over her as she shrank back against the cushions in her chair. 'Unfortunately, I have yet to discover the exact location of the jewels and the gold which you have stolen. So, I suggest that it would be *very* sensible of you to tell me where you have

hidden them—*and as quickly as possible*!' he added
menacingly through clenched teeth.

'Jewels? Gold . . . ?' She blinked up at him in bewilderment. 'The . . . the only jewellery I know about
are the earrings and brooch which I was wearing when
the police found me after the accident. And—er—this
ring, of course,' she added nervously, glancing down
at the gold wedding-band about her finger.

'Do not try my patience too far!' he hissed savagely. 'This farce about you having lost your memory
must now *cease*! I want to know what you have done
with my family's heirlooms—over two million English
pounds' worth of emerald and diamond jewellery
which, together with a large number of gold krug-
errands, has been stolen from the safety deposit box
in my bank, here in Lisbon?'

Tiffany stared up at him in open-mouthed astonishment. To say that he had obviously lost his temper
was a complete understatement. Zarco was absolutely
livid!

Since she was almost numb with terror as his wrath
broke over her frightened figure, it seemed useless to
try and explain that she knew nothing about any
missing jewels or gold. She didn't even know what a
krugerrand looked like, for heaven's sake!

Tiffany was totally bemused by Zarco's colossal and
overwhelming loss of temper, and it was some time
before she could make head or tail of his extraordinary accusation.

It wasn't easy to understand exactly what had happened—mostly because he kept breaking off to swear
violently beneath his breath. However, by the time he
began to simmer down, she'd managed to grasp most
of the salient points. If only half of what he said was

true, she could only be deeply thankful that she *wasn't* Maxine dos Santos!

It seemed that the agents, hired by Zarco, had produced clear evidence of his wife's involvement in the theft of both the gold coins and a fabulous, almost priceless collection of diamond and emerald jewellery, which had been in his family for generations. Zarco was also claiming that it had been a well-thought-out theft, which had required a considerable amount of forward planning.

'I will admit it was a clever scheme—what, I believe, the Americans would call a scam,' he growled through clenched teeth. And Tiffany had to admit that it sounded as if his wife had gone to some considerable lengths in order to steal the jewels.

While Zarco had been away on business in Brazil, Maxine had apparently left their house in England and flown secretly to Portugal. On arriving in Lisbon, she'd paid the first of many visits to Zarco's bank, in the Baixa area of the city, where she had opened an account in her own name. Maxine had also asked if she could have a safety deposit box, in which to keep some important documents—apparently for the purchase of a large house outside the city.

Making several visits to the bank vaults, to take out and replace the 'documents', Maxine had become well known and easily recognised by the official in charge. So, when she had arrived one afternoon just before the bank was due to close, and had asked the man if she could also transfer some of the 'documents' from her own safety deposit box to that of her husband, it had not occurred to the bank official to have any doubts about the wisdom of letting her do so. After all, the Senhor Marquês dos Santos was an old and valued client.

'The man does remember you carrying a large wicker shopping bag,' Zarco told her with a harsh bark of angry laughter. '*So* convenient—after you'd emptied *my* safety deposit box—for concealing within its depths all the antique jewellery and gold coins!'

And his wife had also, it seemed, planned the timing of her theft very carefully. Stealing the jewellery just before the bank closed on a Thursday afternoon—with the next day, Friday, being a bank holiday to celebrate the Day of Liberation—no one was likely to discover the robbery until well after the weekend.

'I have never denied that you are a clever and devious woman, Maxine,' he told her grimly. 'But in this case, I think you were perhaps just a little *too* clever for your own good! Was it a case of thieves falling out?' he demanded. 'Is that why you were seen struggling with a man and woman beside the cliff, only one day after you'd stolen the jewels? Is *that* why you received such a heavy blow to your head...?'

'I... I'm not even capable of planning such a complicated plot—let alone clever enough to carry it out!' she cried helplessly.

'You lie!'

The tension of the sudden silence which had fallen on the small hospital room was so thick and heavy that she could almost cut it with a knife, Tiffany thought faintly, her heart thudding and pounding like a heavy drum. The expression on Zarco's face as he paced up and down the floor sent frantic shivers of fear rippling down her spine; a dire warning—as if she needed any such reminder!—of the folly in continuing to defy this apparently invincible man.

Drawing on her pitiful reserves of strength, she made one last effort to convince him. 'I don't... I *really* don't know what your wife did, because I am quite certain that I am *not* Maxine. In fact I've now remembered ... I now know that my name is Tiffany Harris, and——'

Zarco's heavy snort of anger cut across her words as she haltingly tried to protest her innocence.

'—and I don't know *anything* about any jewels—heirlooms or otherwise,' she added breathlessly as his harsh features grew dark with rage and fury.

'*Stop lying to me!*'

She cried out in alarm as he suddenly grabbed hold of her hands, swiftly pulling her trembling figure upright from the chair. Quickly clasping hold of both her wrists with one hand and taking hold of her chin with the other, he drew her closer as his tanned fingers forced her head up towards him.

She felt as though her mind was being probed by a viciously sharp laser. Standing so close, she was aware of the angry flush beneath the tanned skin covering his high cheekbones and formidable jawline; her eyes gazing helplessly at the cruel, sensual curve of his mouth.

'You are merely wasting my time,' he drawled with grim, silky menace. 'It is pointless to continue to deny that you stole the jewels and the gold—especially when I have such a large mountain of evidence to prove that you did!'

'Somebody...somebody may have raided your bank deposit box—but I promise you it wasn't *me!*' she wailed. 'I'm just not capable of doing something like that. You're making a *terrible* mistake!' she added in a tremulous whisper as his fingers tightened threateningly about her chin.

There was a long silence, her eyelashes fluttering nervously beneath his fierce gaze as he drew her tightly against his tall figure. She could feel his long, muscular thighs touching her own, and, despite her very real fear of this dangerous man, it was some moments before her bewildered mind was able to recognise the nervous, quivering response feathering through her trembling body.

Oh, *no*! Surely, she couldn't be *sexually* attracted to this man...? she asked herself wildly. It simply wasn't possible—she must have totally lost her mind! But then, of course, she *had* temporarily lost part of her mind, she quickly reminded herself. Although it seemed that Zarco, too, was beginning to doubt his own sanity.

'I must be losing my head!' he growled softly, gazing down into the wide blue eyes of the girl trapped within his arms.

Totally confused from the mental battering she had received over the past half-hour, and bemused by her inexplicable response to the dark attraction of this man whom she feared and hated, Tiffany was hardly prepared for what happened next.

Barely able to understand what was happening, she found herself crushed against his hard chest, his arms tightening like a vice about her slender body. The fingers gripping her jaw swiftly slipped down to clasp the back of her neck, holding her head firmly beneath him. His dark eyes flashed a glittering warning, and then his mouth came crushing down like a weapon against her lips, the relentless pressure almost paralysing her.

She was breathless, mentally stunned before the realisation of what was happening really hit her, so it was some seconds before she began to make a feeble effort to escape from his cruel embrace. She tried to cry out, but, even as she parted her lips, she realised that she was making a grave mistake as he took advantage of her foolishness, the hot exploration of his tongue a savage invasion of her shattered senses.

Her first strangled cry had given way to an inaudible moan. She could hardly breathe, and, despite her feeble attempts to struggle free, she knew that it was hopeless. He was clearly possessed of a strength she couldn't possibly combat. The arm clasping her so tightly began to slide slowly down her body, pressing her even closer to his hard frame, and she was once again conscious of a strong tide of erotic, sexual awareness within herself, which even his determined assault had not extinguished. It was even more disturbing to realise that Zarco dos Santos was also a victim of this inexplicable attraction between them, the hard arousal of his own body clearly underlining the fact.

And then she found herself released from her torment. She lay limply in his arms, and it was some moments before she could force her eyelids open, blinking dazedly up at the man towering over her.

His dark glittering eyes were guarded, staring down at her with a searching and watchful expression from beneath his heavy eyelids.

'You...you've just assaulted me!' she gasped, struggling to raise a hand to her bruised, swollen lips.

'It is hardly an assault if a man should decide to kiss his wife,' Zarco told her dismissively. 'And maybe it is something I should have done long ago, hmm?'

'But I'm *not* your wife!' she cried huskily.

'*Cale-se*. Be quiet!' he rasped, his temper almost flaring up out of control once more. And then, after a fierce internal struggle, he continued in a calmer voice, 'I don't see how you can have it both ways. Either you have *not* lost your memory—in which case you must know perfectly well where you have hidden the jewels, or you *have* temporarily lost your mind,' he drawled silkily, 'and it is, therefore, merely a question of my waiting until you have regained it, once again.'

He shrugged his broad shoulders when he saw that she wasn't capable of making any reply. 'In either case, I will soon have the answer. The doctors inform me that they are willing to let you leave the hospital tomorrow. And once we are back at my house in England...' He laughed. 'I do not foresee any difficulty in forcing you to tell me what I want to know!'

Her trembling legs gave way beneath her as his blood-curdling, evil laugh echoed around the small room. And she would have fallen if he hadn't tightened his grip on her slim figure.

'Let me go! Please—*please* let me go...!' she sobbed helplessly, ashamed to find herself losing all control, and crying out with terror as he quickly scooped her up in his arms.

Swearing violently under his breath, Zarco frowned down at the tearful, struggling girl in his arms. And then he spun around on his heel, walking swiftly over to place her surprisingly gently down on the bed.

'I'm not Maxine. I know I'm not!' she wept, still feeling totally shattered by his determined, fierce assault of only a few moments ago. 'My name is Tiffany Harris—and this is all a t-terrible, *terrible* m-mistake!'

Seemingly deaf to her tearful cry of protest, Zarco studied her in silence for a moment, before reaching over to press a bell for the nurse.

'See to my wife!' he demanded imperiously as the nurse swiftly responded to his call. 'And since I have permission to remove her from here, tomorrow,' he added, ignoring the presence of the sobbing girl on the bed as he strode towards the door, 'I expect her to be up and dressed when I collect her, tomorrow morning.'

She was shattered by her confrontation with Zarco, and her pathetic attempts to interest either the doctor, or the nurses, in what she feared was a clear case of kidnapping proved hopeless.

The nurses, although warm and caring girls, simply didn't have the clout to interfere with the doctor's decision—even if they had believed her story, which they clearly didn't. As for the doctor, while he was very kind and compassionate in his firm belief that she was indeed suffering from amnesia, he nevertheless felt that her best chance of recovery lay in accompanying her husband back home to England.

'O Senhor Marquês tells me that he has a *quinta* in England—a very large house and very quiet. It will be good for you to have peace and serenity, yes?'

No—it won't! she wanted to scream out loud. But, of course, she didn't. There was no point, she realised with dismay, in protesting any further. Not when the whole of the hospital seemed to be bowing and scraping before the Senhor Marquês.

She might have lost most of her memory, Tiffany thought glumly. But she had no difficulty in recalling the well-known saying, 'Everyone loves a lord!' It might be a republican country—but, as far as she could see, members of the aristocracy were still living high, wide and handsome in Portugal!

And, as if to complete her misery, even Emily Pargeter turned out to have feet of clay—falling a willing victim to Zarco's charm.

Calling in to see her the next morning, the elderly woman arrived just as Tiffany was being helped into the clothes for her journey.

'I didn't realise you were leaving us quite so soon, dear,' Emily murmured, raising an eyebrow as she viewed the ultra-smart white raw silk suit which the young girl was wearing.

When Tiffany explained that she was due to be collected by Zarco, and was being forced to return with him to his large house in England, Emily was most sympathetic.

'Although maybe it's for the best?' she concluded reassuringly. 'With lots of rest in the peaceful English countryside, I'm sure that you'll soon be able to remember far more about your past life.'

'I certainly hope so!' Tiffany said fervently, before telling her friend about the loss of the jewellery and gold from Zarco's bank—and how there was no way she could prove that she hadn't planned and carried out such an audacious robbery,

'Just as there's no way I can prove that I *know* I've never worn anything like this before,' she added, grimacing down at the *very* short skirt, which seemed to come halfway up her thighs. 'This outfit was apparently delivered here, for me to wear to the airport. And while it may well be the height of fashion, I'm quite certain that I've *never* possessed a garment made by Yves Saint Laurent. And I never wear white. With my pale skin, it makes me look totally washed out.'

The elderly woman smiled. 'Well, dear, I think you look very nice. Although I'd agree that maybe it's not a very practical colour in which to travel.'

'Thank you for trying to be tactful.' Tiffany gave a heavy sigh as she turned to look at herself in the mirror, raising a nervous hand to the thick bandage which was still wound about her head. 'Quite honestly, I don't need anyone to tell me that I look like an advertisement for keeping death off the roads!' she muttered glumly.

'Come on, dear, cheer up!' Emily told her. 'And what an exciting story you've just told me,' she added, clearly more interested in the tangled web which the young girl found herself than in the colour of her clothing. 'I can't remember hearing about anything *so* extraordinary before. And I hear from the nurses that your husband is *such* a handsome man, too!'

Tiffany looked at her in astonishment. 'What does it matter whether he's good-looking or not? The fact is that he's a thoroughly awful, terrifying man who scares me rigid. Quite honestly,' she added gloomily, 'I reckon he's *just* the sort of person who'd pull the wings off poor little butterflies!'

Gaining considerable satisfaction at tearing the character of her loathsome so-called husband to pieces, Tiffany was distracted by the sound of a low cough. Whirling round, she was startled to see the tall, dominant figure of Zarco lounging casually in the open doorway of her room.

How much had he heard? Tiffany felt quite sick for a moment, her knees trembling weakly as he gave her a tight, thin smile; a smile not reflected in his glittering dark eyes, which contained no amusement whatsoever.

'I'm sorry to disappoint you—but it's a very long time since I behaved in such a disgusting manner towards "poor little butterflies"—I certainly cannot remember ever doing so,' he drawled coolly, before moving smoothly forward to greet Emily Pargeter.

'I understand that you have been kindness itself to my dear wife,' he murmured, giving the elderly woman a warm and engaging smile as he gallantly lifted her hand to his lips. 'However, you may rest assured that she will have the very best of care on our return to England.'

If she hadn't been feeling so furiously angry and upset, Tiffany might have laughed out loud at the glazed expression on Emily's face; an expression echoed by that of the young nurse. But if Tiffany had ever had a sense of humour, it had now completely deserted her. Fuming with rage, she found herself having to watch the dreadful man spinning a web of outrageous charm, in which he was clearly ensnaring her only friend in Lisbon.

Poor Emily seemed to have been totally swept off her feet, eagerly requesting details of exactly where Zarco's house was located, before eventually pulling herself together and declaring that it was time she went.

'Goodbye, dear,' the elderly woman murmured as she came over to give Tiffany a hug. 'He really *is* handsome—and *so* charming!' she whispered in the girl's ear, giving her a beaming smile before hurrying from her room.

Emily Pargeter had been quite right when she'd suggested that a white raw silk suit would be unsuitable for the rigours of everyday travel. However, after having been driven to the airport by Zarco's chauffeured limousine, speeding across the tarmac to where his private jet was waiting for take-off, Tiffany realised that for the seriously rich such details were irrelevant. Unfortunately, she was given little time for speculation about Zarco's wealth as, after handing her carefully out of the vehicle, he once again swept her off her feet.

'Put me down!' she gasped, trying to struggle free
of his embrace as he carried her lightly up the steps
and into the aircraft.

She hated being held so close to him. Strangely
fearful of the strong, firm arms clasping her to his
rock-hard body, she was acutely conscious of the same
breathlessness—the very same *frisson* of excitement
and longing which she'd felt yesterday, in the hospital.

Bewildered by her reaction to a man whom she was
so certain she actively disliked, Tiffany found herself
being lowered down into a comfortable seat. Leaning
back and closing her eyes, she meekly allowed him to
fasten her seatbelt. When she opened her eyes again,
it was to see Zarco having a few brief words with his
pilot, before moving towards a large executive-type
desk, which seemed to be firmly secured in place.

Watching as he shrugged off the dark grey jacket
of his expensively cut suit, to reveal the broad
shoulders and strong, muscular shape of his tall body,
Tiffany realised that she knew absolutely nothing
about this man.

It was undoubtedly a waste of time, but as she
studied the angular bones of his face, covered by a
firm and deeply tanned skin, she had the distinct impression that such wealth as he possessed—and he was
obviously as rich as Croesus—was not solely due to
an aristocratic inheritance. Even if this particular man
had been born a pauper, she was oddly certain that
his sheer aggressiveness, his obvious ability to lead
and command, would have taken him to the top of
any company or international corporation.

Engaged in idle speculation on the forces which lay
behind his powerful, ruthless personality, she suddenly realised that Zarco had turned his gaze in her
direction. The searchlight of his glittering dark eyes

bored into hers, as if searching for an elusive answer. For a moment it seemed as though the air were charged with electricity: a crackling tension that flashed between their still figures. But then the extraordinary sensation which had temporarily paralysed her body quickly drained away as he gave a slight shrug, and began to concentrate on the papers laid out on the desk before him.

Feeling extraordinarily tired and exhausted, Tiffany must have slept through most of the journey, moving like a sleep-walker through the formalities of London airport, before accompanying Zarco in yet another chauffeur-driven car to his country house by the Thames, in Berkshire.

As the vehicle came to a halt on the gravelled forecourt of Norton Manor, Tiffany realised how much she'd been subconsciously hoping that the house would seem familiar. But, as she was helped from the car and took a faltering step towards the front door, she was swept by a sudden wave of deep depression.

Against all common sense, she'd hoped to be able to discover *some* point of contact with Zarco's wife: how else could she have been found dressed in Maxine's clothes, and wearing the other woman's jewellery? But she had no recollection in her mind of this beautiful timber-framed medieval manor house, whose ancient diamond-shaped windows sparkled in the late afternoon sun. In fact, as she entered the large oak-panelled hall, fragrant with the smell of beeswax and bowls of fresh spring flowers, it all seemed desperately unfamiliar. As did the stranger, who bustled forth from the nether regions of the large house to greet Zarco with a beaming smile.

Weary and bewildered as she was, Tiffany instantly realised that the middle-aged woman—whom she subsequently learned was Amy Long, the house-keeper—was definitely no friend of hers. After effusively welcoming the master of the house and informing him that tea was laid in the drawing-room, Amy Long's smile faded as she turned to coolly enquire whether 'Madam would care to rest after the journey?'

Wilting beneath the chilly, hostile gaze of the other woman, Tiffany instinctively turned for protection to the tall figure standing beside her. After a swift glance at the frightened, nervous expression on the girl's pale face, Zarco smoothly informed the housekeeper that his wife was very tired, and would undoubtedly welcome a soothing cup of tea just as soon as he'd carried her upstairs to her bedroom.

Astounded to discover that Zarco was capable of being kind and considerate, Tiffany meekly allowed herself to be carried upstairs. Moving down a wide passage, Zarco entered a large, beautifully decorated room which was dominated by an elegant four-poster bed. As he lowered her gently down on to the thick pile of the pale cream carpet, Tiffany's eyes widened as she gazed about her. Through the open door of the en-suite bathroom, she could see the gleam of gold taps reflected in the shining mirrors which appeared to line the walls. Her stupefied gaze absorbed the shimmering pale green silk curtains edging the windows, the same material being used for the intricate drapery on the elegant pale satinwood columns of the bed, before she shook her head in disbelief.

'Are you feeling any pain?' he asked, still keeping an arm lightly about her slim, obviously drooping figure.

'No... I'm just feeling exhausted, that's all,' she muttered, her weary body filled with a deep longing to climb between the sheets of the wide, comfortable-looking bed. And then, as her weary brain absorbed the significant fact that it was a *double* bed, she could feel icy shivers of apprehension racing up and down her spine.

'Am I expected to...?' She gulped. 'I mean, do we—er——?' As she hesitated he gave a low rumble of sardonic laughter.

'No, my dear wife, we do *not* share the same bedroom,' he drawled, his sensual lips tightening as she visibly sagged with relief.

'If you really *are* suffering from amnesia,' he continued coldly, 'maybe I should inform you that we have not slept together since the date of our wedding.'

The harsh bitterness lying beneath his terse words seemed to reverberate around the room, almost battering her travel-weary body.

'I didn't know... I didn't realise...' she muttered, a flush stealing over her pale cheeks as she stared fixedly down at the carpet.

'Can it be that you are feeling some remorse?' he drawled sardonically, before turning to walk back across the room towards the open doorway. 'It is, of course, far too late for that. Especially, as you know very well, Maxine—or whatever name you now wish to call yourself—that I lead quite another—er—private life, in Brazil!'

As he closed the door quietly behind him, the only sound to disturb the deep silence of the large house was the fading echo of his wry, sardonic laughter.

CHAPTER FOUR

AFTER waving goodbye to Dr Granville, who'd been paying his weekly visit to see her, Tiffany was about to turn back into the house when she hesitated for a moment.

It was one of those rare, gloriously warm mornings in late May. And since it seemed almost a crime not to be outside enjoying the sunshine, she couldn't resist the temptation to explore the grounds of Norton Manor.

From what little information she'd been able to gather over the past two weeks, it appeared that the house had been built by a Richard Norton in the fifteenth century—mainly from the proceeds gained by lending money to both sides engaged in fighting the English War of the Roses. The timber-framed medieval house had continued to be owned by the Norton family through subsequent generations, remaining virtually untouched until it was inherited by the last member of the family, Charlotte Norton.

Strolling slowly past an ancient tithe barn and a large round dovecot, set in a red-bricked wall surrounding the garden, Tiffany found herself wishing that she knew more about Charlotte Norton. The English girl had been Zarco dos Santos's first wife—before dying at a tragically young age, shortly after the birth of her son.

It was no good asking Zarco, of course. During the first week following their return from Lisbon, he had barely been able to bring himself to be polite to her.

And, since he'd been away in Portugal on business for the last six days, her only source of information had been Amy Long, the far from friendly housekeeper at Norton Manor.

However, from what she had learned, it seemed that Charlotte had been an only child of elderly parents. After studying Spanish and Portuguese at university, she had decided to take a year off following her studies to visit Brazil. And it was there that she had met and married her husband—a marriage which had, apparently, been violently opposed by her mother and father. 'Miss Charlotte was always headstrong,' the housekeeper had told her with a wistful smile, explaining how Sir Richard and Lady Norton had eventually forgiven their daughter, travelling to Brazil to visit their new grandson and his mother shortly before she had died.

'And what about my—er—husband?' Tiffany had asked, having temporarily given up the unequal struggle to prove that she *wasn't* married to Zarco.

'Oh, he and Sir Richard got on like a house on fire! Which is why Miss Charlotte's father left him this house when he died—and then to be passed on in turn to young Carlos. Mind you, the Marquês being a real live aristocrat helped, of course,' Amy had laughed. 'Old Sir Richard always was a right snob! But my Miss Charlotte's marriage was a true love match—not like some "arrangements" I don't care to mention!' the housekeeper had added, giving Tiffany a scornful glance before bustling off about her duties.

With a heavy sigh, Tiffany sank down on to a carved stone bench, set against the warm brick wall surrounding the herb garden. The housekeeper, who had been at Norton Manor since she was a young girl, ran the house like clockwork. Assisted by three or four ladies from the nearby village, who came to dust and polish every day, Amy didn't tolerate any interference in the running of the manor house—and Tiffany's assurance that she was happy to leave everything to the older woman had been received in stony silence and with considerable scepticism. While Amy ran the house, her husband Tom acted as Zarco's chauffeur, general factotum and also as butler, when the need arose. The immaculate grounds surrounding the house seemed to have an army of gardeners constantly manicuring the lawns, making sure that no weed dared show its face in the flowerbeds. In fact, Tiffany told herself wryly, Zarco's annual bill for the upkeep of this house and grounds was probably as much as most people earned in a lifetime!

None of which, she quickly reminded herself, solved the problem of what on earth she was going to do about Amy Long. It was, of course, quite understandable that the housekeeper might resent Zarco's second wife—especially since the older woman had known and loved Charlotte Norton from childhood. However, it had become obvious that, although Maxine had lived in this house for some time, she had not succeeded in gaining the housekeeper's respect.

In fact, Tiffany thought gloomily, Maxine seemed to have had one really outstanding talent—that of upsetting and alienating *everyone* with whom she came into contact! It was deeply depressing to find herself trapped by a close physical resemblance to such a disagreeable and thoroughly unpleasant woman. And her own clear failure to recall any trace of her past life in this house—and how could she, when she'd never been here?—seemed to have Zarco and all the medical experts completely stumped.

She certainly had to give Zarco 'A' for effort, Tiffany thought grimly. In the week following her arrival at Norton Manor, at least four days had been spent going back and forth to London. Refusing to listen to her pleas that she wasn't Maxine, and that each passing day she was recalling more and more of her life as Tiffany Harris, Zarco had dragged her from the expensive consulting-rooms of one specialist to another.

At his insistence, she had been put through hypnosis, psychoanalysis and psychotherapy, until she was heartily sick of the sight of Harley Street! And all to no avail. In the beginning, she had thought it would be easy to convince the medical men of her true identity—especially since, as the doctor in Lisbon had promised, she was remembering more and more of her past life as Tiffany Harris. But, as soon as Zarco had followed her into the various consulting-rooms, his total and certain conviction that she was his wife put everything back to square one! After all, if a man didn't know his wife—who did? And Tiffany's increasingly desperate assertion that she *wasn't* Maxine had merely been put down to amnesia caused by the blow to her head.

Every expert seemed to have a different theory about why she couldn't recall her married life with her husband. A particularly ingenious explanation seemed to centre upon a famous case in America, where a woman was found to have at least three completely different personalities, and whose story had featured in a famous movie. However, it wasn't until her last visit to a surprisingly friendly psychiatrist that Zarco had finally begun to accept the truth: his wife really had no memory of their past life together.

'We have not achieved much success, I'm afraid,' Dr Watkins had told Zarco, when he'd entered the consulting-room after her visit. 'It's a very interesting story your wife has to tell, about her life as the wife of a professional tennis player, and——'

'Nonsense!' Zarco had snapped irritably. 'She knows nothing about tennis, and has always been completely uninterested in any form of sporting activity,' he'd added firmly. 'I wish to know when, in your professional opinion, my wife will recover her memory. And, in particular, how soon she may recall the events leading up to her injury.'

Dr Watkins had shrugged. 'I fully expect your wife to eventually recollect most of the details of her childhood, her adolescence and her marriage to you. However, I'm afraid that you must accept the fact that she may never remember what happened in the hours, or even days, before the accident.'

'Never...?' A deep frown had creased Zarco's forehead, his lips tightening with annoyance and frustration. 'Surely there must be some way to extract that information from my wife? Some way of unlocking her memory?'

'There are plenty of other experts in London,' the doctor had told him. 'However, they will all tell you the same thing: your wife has temporary amnesia. While she *may* recollect what or who caused the blow to her head, I think you must face the fact that it is very likely that she won't be able to; that the details of what happened will be lost forever.'

Zarco had remained silent for most of the journey back to Norton Manor, his expression grim and forbidding as he steered the pearl-grey Aston Martin V8 down the motorway.

'It seems I *must* accept what the doctors say,' he'd grated, his harsh tones at last breaking the tense silence. 'But I am *not* abandoning the search to find out what happened in Portugal. My agents will continue to track down your movements during those weeks—and back through your past life, if necessary—until I discover the truth.'

'Good luck!' she'd muttered wearily, leaning back on the red leather head-rest. Nervously closing her eyes at the speed of the fast sports car—the one of Zarco's vehicles which he clearly preferred to drive himself—Tiffany had been just too tired to care *what* he did.

However, it had slowly become obvious, over the next few days, that Zarco had finally accepted her total inability to recall their life together. There had been no more visits to London to see various specialists, and she'd been left alone to recover her strength under the care of Dr Grenville, the local general practitioner.

Thanks to his no-nonsense approach, she was able to discard the heavy bandage, not even needing a plaster on her wound, which was apparently healing very well.

'Just relax, take it easy and I think you'll find that everything sorts itself out very soon,' he'd told her breezily this morning, before arranging to see her in his surgery in a week's time.

It wasn't the wound at the top of her head which had been worrying Tiffany so much as the fact that her hair had been looking such a mess. No wonder Zarco could hardly bear to look at her, his lips curling in distaste whenever his dark, glittering eyes glanced in her direction. And right up until the day after he'd left, on his business trip to Portugal, when she'd been at last able to throw away the hideous bandage, Tiffany had been miserably aware that, with her blonde hair having been roughly chopped into different lengths, she had indeed looked a perfect fright!

Determined to keep up a brave, defiant stance in front of Zarco—although it was clearly a waste of time, since he seemed determined to avoid her like the plague—Tiffany had, of course, spent many hours weeping disconsolately in the privacy of her bedroom. So it had been doubly mortifying when Zarco had appeared unexpectedly in her room the day before he'd left, and discovered her tearfully regarding herself in the mirror.

'Go away!' she'd howled, burying her face in her hands.

'What is wrong? Are you ill?'

'It's my hair—it looks *so* awful!' she'd sobbed through her fingers, desperately wishing that he would go away and leave her in peace.

But, expecting to hear the sound of the door closing behind him, she'd been startled to feel the light touch of his hand on her miserably hunched shoulder.

'I merely came to tell you that I will be going away for a few days to Lisbon, on business,' she'd heard him say quietly. 'As for your hair—that is a matter which can easily be remedied,' he'd added, giving her a surprisingly gentle pat on the shoulder before leaving the room.

Deciding that she must have imagined the note of kindness and concern in his voice, Tiffany had been astounded, on the day following his departure, to receive a visit from a man claiming to be Maxine's London hairdresser.

'Your husband asked me to call and see what I could do with your hair,' the willowy young man said, informing her that he was called Vernon. 'I told him it was going to cost a bomb—dragging me down from London, like this...' Vernon grumbled before giving a high, falsetto shriek of horror. 'Good heavens, ducky! What *have* you done to your hair?'

Stunned by the stranger's unexpected and bizarre appearance—she didn't recall ever having seen a man wearing a pair of long, dangling earrings before—Tiffany haltingly began to explain why her hair had been cut into different lengths.

'That *divine*, macho husband of yours mentioned that you had a cut on the head. But who's been dying your hair? Have you been a *naughty* girl, and visited another hairdresser?' he queried, mincing across the carpet towards her.

'No—I——'

'Hang about!' Vernon exclaimed, quickly dropping his camp tone of voice as he lifted a lock of her hair, running it through his fingers. 'What on earth is going on?' he frowned. 'This isn't your hair...or, to be more precise, it's not the hair *I've* been looking after for the past two years!'

Tiffany could have hugged him. Here—at last—was proof positive that she wasn't Maxine!

It took her some time to explain the complicated situation and how, incredible as it might seem, a terrible mistake had been made over her identity. And even if she wasn't Maxine, would Vernon *please* do something about her dreadful-looking hair?

Deciding that he was faced with an interesting challenge, the hairdresser said that he would see what he could do. And, well over an hour later, they were both happy to agree that he had done very well.

Fascinated to hear what details she could tell him about the blow to her head, Vernon revealed himself to be a thoroughly sensible, down-to-earth Londoner. 'With a wife, two kids and several brothers and sisters to support, I only do the ''Hello, duckie!'' bit because it's good for business,' he told her with a grin, taking considerable care to achieve a style which would go some way to disguising the wound on her head.

'Actually, I think you look rather good with short hair,' he murmured, carefully brushing the now soft, slightly wavy gold hair into a shining cap about her head. 'It looks like you're in a real bind, although I suppose there are worse fates in life than having to live a life of luxury!' he added with a grin, stepping back to view his new creation. 'All the same...I can't help wondering what on earth has happened to Maxine.'

Delighted by the dramatic improvement in her appearance, Tiffany hadn't taken too much notice of Vernon's remark, at the time. But now, as she sat here in the herb garden, relishing the warmth of the mid-morning sun, Tiffany recalled his query. It was, she realised, a question she should have asked herself long before now. Because, if *she* was here at Norton Manor—where on earth was Maxine?

Everyone who'd been in close contact with Zarco's wife seemed to be in agreement that she was, or had been, a deeply unpleasant woman. Moreover, it didn't seem as though Maxine had any friends—certainly no acquaintances had either called or phoned to say hello during the past two weeks. All of which seemed very strange.

Recalling Zarco's caustic, unhappy bark of laughter about his wife, on the night of her arrival here at Norton Manor, Tiffany totally failed to understand what he could find amusing about a marriage which, according to him, had been no marriage at all. And, if it had been so awful, why hadn't Maxine run away years ago? Nothing, not even her dressing-room, which appeared to be filled to overflowing with *couture* garments, designer shoes and exquisite lingerie, could possibly compensate for what must have been a thoroughly miserable, desolate existence.

And what about Zarco? Every time she thought about the problem, Tiffany kept coming up against the same massive stumbling block. *Why* was Zarco so certain that she was Maxine?

Even if he didn't share his wife's bed, Zarco must have spent a great deal of time with her, right? But, although she might look like Maxine—and everyone seemed convinced that she did—Tiffany was certain that their character and personality must be very different. So, why hadn't he noticed that fact? After all, there was no one closer to a married woman, or who ought to know her better, than her husband.

As the arguments swayed back and forth in her brain, Tiffany gave a heartfelt sigh of despondency. She couldn't blame Zarco for not liking his wife—especially since everyone else seemed to detest the woman! But she had to admit that there were times when he had been surprisingly kind and considerate. The way he'd rescued her, when she'd first arrived at Norton Manor, and been upset by the housekeeper's chilly reception, had been really thoughtful. And his sympathetic understanding of her feminine despair and misery about the state of her hair had been equally unexpected. What was more, Zarco hadn't just taken pity on her obvious distress—he'd done something about the problem. Arranging the visit of a hairdresser had been a kind gesture, and one which she *must* try to remember the next time he was being particularly nasty or aggressive.

Tiffany gave a heavy sigh as she felt the light breeze rustling through her soft curls. As much as she might want to, it was no good trying to fool herself. Zarco was always going to be a hard, tough and ruthless man—a fierce, dangerous leopard who wasn't likely to ever change his spots!

As she recalled just how fierce and dangerous he could be, Tiffany could feel a deep flush spreading over her pale cheeks. Goodness knows, she'd done her best to forget the extraordinary, upsetting way in which he had treated her in the hospital.

Although she was remembering more and more every day, maybe it was because her memory was so blank that her brain seemed to have nothing else to do but run a constant, perpetual repetition of the embarrassing episodes. It was just as though someone had pushed the continuous play-back button on a video recorder. Unfortunately, whatever the reason, she couldn't seem to blot out of her memory the touch of his tanned fingers on her breasts, nor the heady warmth and sensual excitement of his mouth and tongue, when he'd clasped her so tightly in his arms.

Almost gasping at the intense, twisting pain which suddenly scorched through her body, Tiffany clenched her eyes tightly shut and tried to fill her lungs with a deep, steadying breath. What on earth was *wrong* with her? She didn't need to remind herself of how much she disliked Zarco dos Santos. Even with two casual acts of kindness to his credit, he was still someone who ought to carry a large, clearly visible warning: 'Beware! This Man is Dangerous!'

So, she must...she really *must* try to forget what had happened. It had obviously meant nothing to Zarco. He'd certainly never attempted to repeat the actions which, she was quite sure, had been meant as a calculated, deliberate punishment towards a wife he clearly hated. And, if she'd found the incidents profoundly devastating, it must have been due to her obviously weak state of mind and body, following the blow to her head.

Preoccupied with trying to rationalise and explain away her inexplicable, emotional response to Zarco, Tiffany hadn't realised that she was no longer alone in the herb garden.

Distracted by a slight sound, she looked up in surprise to see Amy Long picking some mint from a bed in the far corner of the garden. As she watched the plump middle-aged woman gathering a collection of herbs, Tiffany suddenly decided that this was a good opportunity to try and sort matters out with the housekeeper.

Amy had made it plain that she cordially detested Zarco's second wife, but Tiffany saw no reason why *she* should have to suffer just because the two women had loathed one another. And, with Zarco's departure for Portugal, she'd been left very much at the mercy of the housekeeper.

Tiffany felt sure that she'd never had to live with such enmity before: a cold hostility which was making her even more lonely and unhappy than she'd have believed possible. Every friendly approach had been firmly repulsed by the housekeeper, and she was feeling desperately in need of some warm, human companionship.

'Look,' she began, after telling Amy that she wanted a word with her, 'I don't know whether—er—my husband has told you about my accident, in Portugal...?'

'I've heard very little, madam,' the housekeeper told her, in her usual prim and chilly tone of voice.

'Well, I'd like to talk to you about it, and . . . Oh— for heaven's sake, Amy! Won't you *please* sit down and relax?' Tiffany exclaimed with exasperation as the other woman remained standing stiffly in front of her.

'I don't bite. I haven't got an infectious disease. And, since we have to live together in this house, it seems absolutely *crazy* for us not to be friends. Right?'

Obviously startled by the girl's outburst, Amy hesitated for a moment. Then, with a slight shrug of her shoulders, she lowered herself silently down on to the bench.

'Well—that's a start, anyway,' Tiffany sighed, before taking her courage in both hands and launching forth into an explanation of all that had happened to her in Portugal. Nor did she omit the extraordinary story of the theft of Zarco's gold and jewellery from his bank in Lisbon.

'And, just to make the whole thing ten times worse, Amy,' she added helplessly, 'I can't seem to persuade anyone—not even my so-called husband—that there's been a really *terrible* mistake. That I'm *not* that simply awful woman, Maxine dos Santos!'

'Yes, well . . . if what you say is right, you do seem to have a problem!' Amy agreed slowly.

'I have remembered quite a bit about my past life as Tiffany Harris—when I was married to a not very successful professional tennis player, Brian Harris. We spent our life travelling around the world on the tennis circuit, but, unfortunately, I can't remember a thing about Portugal. I don't even know why I was in the country, in the first place. And as for being found up at Sintra . . . ?' She shrugged unhappily. 'I simply don't have a clue what I was doing there. And . . . and because I've lost my memory—there isn't a damned thing I c-can d-do about it!' she wailed, suddenly overcome by an avalanche of deep loneliness, and desperately ashamed at not being able to prevent the hot tears from flowing down her cheeks.

'Now, now. We can't have you crying like this,' the other woman murmured with concern, putting a comforting arm around Tiffany's bowed, quivering shoulders.

'I . . . I'm s-sorry.' The girl raised a trembling hand to brush the tears from her eyes. 'It just . . . well, it's all got on top of me, I suppose,' she muttered, gratefully accepting a handkerchief from Amy and quickly blowing her nose.

'See here,' the housekeeper said, when Tiffany had herself more under control, 'if it's any comfort, I can tell you that I've noticed you *are* very different, since you've returned from abroad. And if you really *aren't* Maxine . . . ?' She paused and frowned as she shook her head. 'Well, I don't know what to think—and that's a fact!'

Tiffany blew her nose again. 'Nor do I. Which is the whole trouble, you see.'

'Hmm . . . yes. I don't know why it never occurred to me that you might *not* be the Marquês's wife. I mean, although we've lived in the house together for some time, she was always very . . .'

'Very nasty and unpleasant?'

'You're not far wrong!' Amy gave a muffled snort of laughter. 'On the other hand, if the Marquês is convinced you really are his wife . . .' She hesitated and shrugged her shoulders.

'That's what has me stumped, too,' Tiffany admitted despondently. 'I've just been telling myself that a man *must* know the woman he's married to. I mean, you can't live *that* close to someone—not without knowing them really well, can you?'

To her horror, she couldn't do anything to stop the helpless tears from beginning to stream down her face once again.

'Now—come on, dear. This isn't going to help, is it?' the older woman said firmly, before suggesting that they go back to the house, and have a nice cup of tea in the kitchen.

Sitting at the large, scrubbed pine table and sipping the hot sweet liquid, Tiffany realised it was a tremendous relief to have been able to tell Amy about her problems. Even if the housekeeper found the situation difficult to understand, she was certainly being very kind and friendly.

'Thanks for listening to me, Amy,' Tiffany told her as she put down her cup. 'Quite honestly, I've been almost out of my mind over this business—except that I don't seem to have much of a mind to be out of!' she added with a wry, unhappy smile.

The housekeeper opened her mouth to say something, and then hesitated for a moment as she turned to take a saucepan off the ultra-modern kitchen range.

'I probably shouldn't say anything,' she muttered, turning back to face Tiffany, 'but you can't live in a house without knowing what's going on—if you see what I mean?'

Tiffany wasn't at all sure that she did see, but she gave the older woman an encouraging nod.

'Well . . .' The housekeeper hesitated again, her cheeks slightly pink as she said in a rush, 'I can tell you that, unlike most married couples, the Marquês and his wife didn't—er—they didn't share a bedroom.'

'Yes, I had gathered that,' Tiffany murmured, her cheeks flushed as she stared down at the table.

'Ah, but what you might *not* know is that they've hardly seen each other over the last few years.'

Tiffany raised her head. 'Really?'

'Madam hated having to live here at the manor; she much preferred her own small, modern apartment in London,' Amy said, pursing her lips in tight disapproval. 'Whenever the Marquês was due to come home after a business trip, that Maxine would skip off to London—quick as a flash!—and not come back here until he'd gone. If you ask me...' the housekeeper dropped her voice '...I'm sure it was an excuse to see that fancy man of hers!'

'A *fancy man*?' Tiffany looked at her with startled eyes. It was the first she'd heard about Maxine's apartment in London, and as for the other woman's boyfriend... 'Surely, with such an attractive husband, she couldn't possibly—er——' She broke off in confusion, a deep flush rising up over her cheeks.

Clearly relishing the opportunity to have a good gossip about a woman she actively disliked, Amy didn't appear to notice the girl's heightened colour.

'Oh, yes! She had the brass nerve to invite him here, once or twice, before the Marquês returned unexpectedly one day, and threw him out. Ooh...the Marquês didn't half lose his temper! I've *never* seen him so angry. "I'm not having that greasy hoodlum in *my* house!" he roared. And she took good care never to invite that Tony Silver to the house again. Mind you, she was always on the phone to him, and...'

Tiffany was only half listening as the housekeeper continued letting her hair down about Maxine's boyfriend.

At the first mention of his name, she'd had a fleeting image of a man turning to face her, his dark swarthy features topped by black curly hair beneath a grey peaked hat. 'You're the boss, lady! All the way to Sintra, huh?' he'd been saying with a wide grin, accompanied by a knowing wink and a slight laugh. It was a brief image, which quickly began fading away before Tiffany could grasp it. But, as she strained to recall the sound of the man's voice, she realised her fragile, shakily built house of cards had just collapsed.

'Mind you, both my husband Tom and I knew that Tony Silver was up to no good—right from the first moment we laid eyes on him!' Amy was saying as she poured another cup of tea.

'What—er——?' Tiffany cleared her throat, which seemed obstructed by a large painful lump. 'What did Tony look like?' she asked breathlessly, unable to meet the housekeeper's eyes, as she stared down at the nervously twisting hands in her lap.

'Well, he was sort of like those American gangsters you see on TV. You know—sort of Italian-looking he was, with lots of black curly hair. *Not* a nice man, at all!' Amy added, her voice heavy with disapproval.

How she managed to finish her cup of tea, or go through the polite motions of thanking the housekeeper, before slowly trailing upstairs to her bedroom, Tiffany had no idea. It was, she realised as she threw herself wearily on to the bed, one of the blackest days of her life. Because, while she knew that she wasn't Maxine, she also now had no doubts that she *had* known Maxine's boyfriend. Although how or where was still a complete mystery. Unfortunately, thanks to the housekeeper's revelations, she could no longer assume that there had been a simple mistake in identification. For her to have known Tony, it must mean that she had also known Maxine. So—even if she couldn't remember a thing about it—maybe she *had* been involved in the theft of Zarco's gold and jewellery, after all...?

Humming quietly to herself, Tiffany scattered a light dusting of flour on to the large marble pastry board. She wasn't going to be able to eat it all herself, of course, but Amy had laughingly agreed to sample her first attempt at salmon *en croute*, when the older woman returned tomorrow from a visit to her married daughter in Oxford.

The development of her new friendship with Amy, and the peace and quiet of the old medieval house, had helped Tiffany to come to terms with the fact that somehow—somewhere—she'd met Maxine's boyfriend, Tony Silver. She still couldn't remember anything about how or why she had been in Portugal, but over the last two days she'd been plagued by recurring visions of the man, the flickering images accompanied by frightening, strange feelings of fear and alarm. However, whatever the true answer might prove to be, there didn't seem to be anything she could do at the present time—no alternative but to try and accept this new life at Norton Manor until she had, hopefully, regained her full memory.

However, her new relationship with Amy Long had proved to be very successful. As had been Tiffany's confession that she couldn't remember knowing how to cook anything but very plain, simple meals—and would the housekeeper please teach her how to produce some interesting recipes? Apparently Maxine had been quite a gourmet, and much given to criticising Amy's efforts, so the older woman had been only too pleased to take on the role of cookery instructor. Tiffany wasn't at all sure how her first solo effort was going to turn out, but she was finding it remarkably soothing to be alone, here in the kitchen, with just a large ginger cat for company.

'Well, if this turns out to be a mess, at least you'll be happy to eat the fish!' she told the cat who was lying curled up by the warm kitchen range. 'And that will make a nice change from the mice, which you keep leaving outside my bedroom door!' she added with a slight laugh, as she carefully rolled out the puff pastry.

'To be found talking to oneself is surely the first sign of madness?'

Tiffany gave a shriek, almost jumping out of her skin at the sudden, totally unexpected sound of the deep voice. Spinning around, she was amazed to see the tall, broad-shouldered figure of Zarco lounging casually in the doorway of the kitchen.

'Oh, my goodness! You gave me *such* a fright!' she gasped, clasping floury hands to her chest, where her heart was thumping and pounding like a kettledrum. 'And I wasn't ... wasn't talking to myself. I was actually talking to the cat,' she muttered, before her cheeks flushed as she realised just how silly she must sound.

'Ah, yes. How is my friend the marmalade cat?' Zarco murmured, bending down to pick up the animal, who had raced across the floor to greet him, excitedly rubbing its back against the man's long legs.

'He's fine,' Tiffany muttered, backing nervously up against the table as Zarco walked slowly towards her, casually holding the cat against one shoulder of his expensive, dark grey suit.

Zarco smiled. 'And what do we have here?' he murmured, coming to a halt and gazing down at the pastry-covered board.

'I was just...I mean...Amy's been teaching me...she's been very kind and...' Tiffany gabbled breathlessly, confused by Zarco's sudden, unexpected return from his business trip to Portugal—*and* his close proximity to her nervous figure.

'I think that I approve of this surprisingly new domestic side to your personality,' he drawled.

'You do...?' she murmured nervously, her attention distracted for a moment as she noticed the ginger cat in his arms beginning to take a keen interest in the salmon, lying on a plate beside the pastry.

'Yes, just as I most definitely approve of your new hairstyle. The colour looks far more natural, too.'

Tiffany swallowed apprehensively, prevented by the hard edge of the kitchen table from backing away any further as he raised a hand to tuck a stray lock of hair behind her ear.

'Yes, well...I've got to have a long talk to you about that—and other things too,' she told him huskily. The warm touch of his fingers on her skin was having a disastrous effect on her nervous system, not only leaving her breathless and with her legs feeling as though they were made of jelly, but also causing her to entirely forget what it was she'd been going to say.

'I look forward to trying out this new recipe of yours.'

'*What*...?' She gazed at him in confusion. The glittering dark eyes beneath their heavy lids were regarding her with some amusement. 'You mean...do you mean that you *actually* want to eat this?'

'Why not?' He raised a dark sardonic eyebrow. 'You aren't intending to poison me, are you?'

'No, of course not!' she retorted indignantly. 'It's just that...well, I've never cooked this recipe before, and so I can't guarantee that it's going to be a success,' she added, dearly wishing that she'd never had the bright idea of asking Amy to teach her *haute cuisine*. Although there wasn't going to be anything very *haute* about this particular piece of *cuisine*—not with the awful man looming over her, like this.

Almost as if he could read her mind, Zarco's mouth twitched in silent humour. 'I'm feeling somewhat travel-stained,' he told her blandly. 'So I think I would like to have a shower and change before we eat. That will not interfere with your—er—production of this dish?'

'No—not at all,' Tiffany told him hurriedly, suddenly finding the atmosphere in the large kitchen very claustrophobic. She couldn't help letting out a gasp of apprehension as he lifted a hand, flinching as if she had been stung when he brushed his fingers lightly across her breasts.

'I am merely removing the flour,' Zarco informed her coolly, ignoring her breathless and flustered protests as he calmly—and taking *far* too long about the job, in her opinion!—proceeded to brush her floury fingerprints from the bodice of her cotton blouse.

'There, that is better,' he murmured, after finishing the job to his satisfaction. 'Although, in future, I would suggest that you ought to wear an apron whenever you decide to do any cooking,' he drawled mockingly, before putting the cat back down on the floor and walking slowly away across the kitchen.

Patronising swine! Tiffany thought, her cheeks pink with embarrassment as she hurriedly turned back to complete her preparations for the meal.

After placing the pastry case containing the salmon into the oven, she quickly dashed upstairs to tidy herself before dinner.

A quick glance at her flour-streaked blouse was enough for Tiffany to know that she must find something else to wear. Slipping out of the garment, she pulled a face as she caught sight of her own reflection in the long, full-length mirror on the wall. Having no alternative to wearing the clothes in the wardrobe, she also had no choice but to clothe herself in Maxine's very expensive thin gauzy lingerie. So thin and transparent, indeed, that her hard, swollen nipples were only too evident through the fine silky material.

That dreadful man! Tiffany glowered at herself as she recalled the cool mockery with which he had viewed her embarrassment at his touch on her breasts. He *must* have known what he was doing to her, and the effect that his fingers would have on her body!

She blushed, turning away from the reflection of just how easily Zarco had aroused her weak flesh. Even now, there seemed little she could do to banish the strange, throbbing, sick excitement in the pit of her stomach. With a low moan she rushed into the bathroom, splashing her face with cold water and roughly towelling it dry, as she desperately tried to pull herself together. But, meeting her own blue eyes in the mirror above the basin, she couldn't escape the sight of their numb, apprehensive dread about the evening which lay ahead of her.

CHAPTER FIVE

TIFFANY took a deep breath and tried to relax her nervously rigid, tense figure. It looked such a peaceful scene—the sparkling crystal glasses and the gleam of the silver cutlery reflected in the glowing, highly polished surface of the antique oak refectory dining table.

But she knew better!

Thanks to Zarco, she'd been in a state of total nervous exhaustion for the past hour, attempting to produce the sort of meal which Amy Long could easily have done with her eyes shut, and one hand tied behind her back! To add insult to injury, the dreadful man was now making her wait until he finished every scrap on his plate before expressing an opinion.

Why on earth had she wanted to learn to cook? It was obviously a completely exhausting pastime—and definitely not one she was in any hurry to repeat. In fact, as far as she was concerned, the sooner Amy took back full control of the kitchen, the better!

It was in the middle of changing her dress that Tiffany had suddenly realised she ought to serve a first course, before the salmon in its pastry case made an appearance. After a muffled shriek of dismay, she'd quickly jumped into the nearest garment in the wardrobe, before dashing back downstairs to the kitchen. And that hadn't been such a good idea, either, she told herself gloomily.

There was nothing wrong with the dress itself—a classically simple design in a shade of deep pink raw silk—but if she'd had more time, Tiffany wouldn't have chosen this particular garment. The thin material of the cross-over bodice clung tightly to her full breasts, and the way Zarco's deeply hooded eyes kept glancing towards the low V-shaped neckline was making her feel distinctly nervous.

Down in the kitchen and glassy-eyed with nerves, she'd stared at the packed shelves of the store cupboard, fervently praying for inspiration, before discovering some tins of beef consommé. After emptying them into a saucepan and adding a hefty slug of sherry, she belatedly realised she hadn't even begun to think about what vegetables to serve with the salmon. Or what they were going to eat for dessert.

Buzzing around like a demented housefly, she had more or less got things under control by the time Zarco had made an appearance.

Claiming that they must celebrate 'this auspicious occasion'—apparently, according to him, it was the first time that his wife had ever deigned to cook him a meal—Tiffany had found herself presented with a large glass of sparkling champagne.

Maybe it was the effect of alcohol on an empty stomach, but as she'd stood in the large, elegant drawing-room, with its french windows open to admit the soft evening air, Tiffany had suddenly felt sick with tension. And not just about the forthcoming meal.

Glancing nervously up through her eyelashes at Zarco's tall figure, she hadn't been able to help noting the length of his legs in the slim-fitting black cords. A matching black cashmere sweater worn over a casual, open-necked shirt seemed to emphasise his deeply tanned complexion. With his black hair still damp from the shower, and combed tightly to his well shaped head, he looked formidable—and very, very dangerous.

Unfortunately, Tiffany was also considerably shaken to find herself thinking that he also looked diabolically attractive! Although she did her best to conceal her instinctive, quivering reaction to his aura of dark sensuality, she wasn't at all sure that she'd succeeded. The searchlight beam of those glittering eyes seemed to be capable of invading her very soul.

How *could* she be so stupid as to feel this way— especially about a man whom she both disliked and distrusted? It was a question which had increasingly dominated her mind throughout the meal, and one to which she couldn't seem to find an answer.

'That was really very good indeed.' Zarco's voice cut into her distraught thoughts now, as he placed his knife and fork down on the empty plate.

'Oh—er—I'm glad you liked it,' she muttered, her tense figure almost sagging with relief. 'Um . . . I thought you might be tired after your journey. So I decided we'd just finish the meal with fruit and cheese,' she told him, trying to put a brave face on the fact that she'd weakly chickened out of trying to produce a glamorous dessert.

'That was very thoughtful of you,' he drawled, rising from his chair at the end of the highly polished table to pour her another glass of wine. 'And what culinary masterpiece would you have produced, if I hadn't been so—er—"tired"?'

After a quick, furtive glance up at the gleaming, sardonic amusement in his eyes, Tiffany knew there was no point in trying to fool him.

'I'm afraid that you'd have been out of luck!' she admitted with a slightly nervous, rueful grin as he returned to the other end of the table. 'To tell you the truth, my cooking hasn't progressed much further than learning how to boil an egg!'

Zarco studied her silently for a moment. Casually leaning back in his red-velvet-upholstered chair, he seemed to be absorbed in his own thoughts as he turned to stare blindly at the heavy crystal wine glass on the table in front of him, slowly revolving its slim stem between his long, tanned fingers.

Driven by her inner fear and anxiety of this daunting man, Tiffany quickly searched back through their previous conversation, seeking some clue to the sudden and oppressive silence which had fallen on the table. But she could think of nothing; nothing that could have upset him in the innocuous, harmless few words which they'd exchanged during the meal.

'I think...' Zarco murmured at last, slowly raising his gaze towards her '... I think that before we go any further with this interesting conversation I would like to get a few of the ground rules sorted out. Am I dining with my dear wife, Maxine, who appears to have forgotten that she did a part-time cordon bleu course, a few years ago?' he enquired smoothly. 'Or are you this apparently mythical creature, "Tiffany", who has just informed me—if I understood her correctly—that she wouldn't know an *oeuf mollet* from her elbow...?'

'My name *is* Tiffany Harris!' she retorted. 'Not only have I remembered a great deal more about my past life, but I'm now sure that I can now prove my true identity!' she added triumphantly. 'I was very grateful to you for sending the hairdresser, Vernon, down here to see me. And Vernon has said he's willing to swear that both the texture and the colour of my hair are *not* Maxine's!'

'Oh, really?' Zarco drawled, his voice heavy with scorn. 'I don't think that a statement by a mere hairdresser is likely to carry much weight, do you?'

Tiffany glared down the table at the handsome man who'd so lightly and cynically dismissed the only piece of hard evidence she'd managed to gather so far. How could she have possibly thought him attractive? In fact, Zarco was thoroughly *hateful*—and for two pins she'd tell him so, she raged silently, desperately trying not to give in to an overwhelming urge to shout and scream, and burst into tears of acute frustration.

'It would seem that I have upset you...?'

'Yes—yes, you most certainly *have*!' she burst out angrily. 'I mean...how would *you* like it, if you woke up one day and discovered that you were married to a man who clearly hated you? That—although you couldn't remember a thing about it—you were being accused of theft and grand larceny? And that, all in all, you appeared to be Public Enemy Number One...?' she demanded bleakly.

'Well, Maxine, I——'

'*Don't call me that*!' she stormed. 'If I've *got* to get used to this new life, I'm insisting that everyone calls me by my own true name!'

Zarco shrugged his broad shoulders. 'Very well, if that is what you wish—er—Tiffany. And yes, I will agree that if, as the doctors tell me, you really have no recollection of our past life together, it must indeed be a very trying circumstance.'

'"*A trying circumstance*"?' she exclaimed incredulously. 'Believe me—that's putting it mildly! You don't have *any* conception of the problem, do you?' She jumped to her feet, glowering down the table at him, her figure rigid with overwhelming rage and fury.

'Sit down,' he commanded brusquely. 'There's no need for any of this——'

'There's every need!' She waved her hands distractedly in the air. 'What do I have to do? How can I get it into your thick head that I'm Tiffany Harris? I can give you the names of my father and mother, and even the date on which I married my husband, Brian Harris. But will you listen? Will you—*hell*!' she yelled at him, her normally slow-to-rise temper by now well out of control.

'There is no need to shout at me,' Zarco said firmly. 'I am well aware that there are some facets of your behaviour which I find difficult to—er—match up with those of my wife.'

'Oh, *great*!' Tiffany raged, his cool, rational words merely adding fuel to her passionate anger and fury. 'The great Zarco dos Santos has *actually* noticed some differences between me and his foul wife? Wow! Big deal!'

His face darkened with anger. 'That's quite enough of this nonsense!'

'That's all it is to you—*nonsense*!' she lashed back huskily, the fierce storm of temper draining away from her trembling figure, almost as fast as it had arisen. 'For goodness' sake, Zarco—can't you admit that you've made a mistake...? Do you *really* have to be s-so b-blind?' she begged tearfully, before taking to her heels and dashing out of the room, running up the long, curving staircase to seek refuge in her bedroom.

Tiffany sat up in the bath, wringing out her sponge to wipe away the last trace of her recent flood of tears. She really must pull herself together, she told herself firmly, leaning over the side of the bath to extract some tissues from her make-up bag, and blowing her nose fiercely. Lying back in the warm water, she stared blindly up through the clouds of steam as she tried to work out what on earth she was going to do.

She was sure that never before had she lost her temper quite so spectacularly. Quite certain that she was, normally, a quiet and reserved sort of person, which might be the reason why she was now feeling so exhausted and shattered at having made such an exhibition of herself, and for the storm of tears which had followed.

However, angry as she was with Zarco, she couldn't entirely blame him for what had happened. Because she had to admit that she'd been in a considerable state of nerves even before they had sat down to the meal. In fact, that meal had been positively her very last attempt to master the art of cooking. She had quite enough problems, without adding the strain and tension of trying to master an unfamiliar branch of science! However, while it was all very well to dismiss the idea of turning herself into a perfect little house-keeper—clearly an aim which she should never have attempted in the first place—there was no escaping the fact that she really must try and leave Norton Manor, as soon as possible.

Although she hadn't anywhere to go, Tiffany knew that she couldn't remain here any longer. For one thing, the thought of more rows and arguments was enough to make her feel ill. And those were bound to arise, since Zarco was obviously determined to continue trying to prove that she was his wife, Maxine. And, however futile it might be, she had no alternative but to continue insisting on her own identity. So . . . what choice had she? As much as she loved this old medieval house, she must leave and try to make a new life for herself—well away from the disturbing influence of Zarco dos Santos. But how she was going to do so, with no money or formal identification, she had absolutely no idea.

The rapidly cooling water of the bath intruded into her distracted thoughts, and, stepping out to envelop herself in a short, warm fleecy towel, she walked slowly through into the bedroom. Only to come to a startled, stumbling halt at the sight of Zarco, calmly sitting in a comfortable chair beside the bed.

'Ah, there you are—at last!' he drawled smoothly.

'Wh-what are you doing in here?' she breathed huskily, nervously clutching the towel around her naked body. 'What do you want?'

He ignored her breathless questions. 'I trust you are feeling somewhat better, and more relaxed after your bath?'

'Yes—er—yes, I'm sorry . . . I don't usually lose my temper,' Tiffany muttered, her cheeks flushed as she stared guiltily down at her bare feet, her toes curling with embarrassment into the thick pile of the carpet.

'That is exactly why I am here. I think that it's time you and I had a long talk,' he stated coolly.

'No, I really don't think . . . there doesn't seem to be any point in——'

'I have decided that we are going to have a long talk,' he repeated firmly. 'And, while I might agree that you look enchanting in that brief towel, I think you might feel more comfortable in something possibly less—er—revealing!' he added in a mocking drawl, his dark eyes glinting with amusement as he viewed her efforts to pull the towel more tightly about her slim figure.

Tiffany could feel a deep tide of crimson flooding over her face and body as she registered the sardonic, cynical amusement in his deep voice. As she told herself later, she really *would* have stood her ground and ordered him out of the bedroom, if she hadn't made the mistake of raising her head to give the hateful man a scornful, withering glance.

Unfortunately, as soon as she viewed Zarco leaning casually back in his chair, idly allowing his eyes to conduct an analytical appraisal of her trembling body—one that began at the top of her head and travelled insolently down over her slim figure to the pink toenails of her bare feet—she was immediately thrown into confusion. With no impulse other than to immediately escape from those insulting dark eyes, she spun around and pulled open a drawer, swiftly grabbing the nearest garment before whisking herself back into the sanctuary of the bathroom.

The damned nerve of the man! she thought angrily, banging the door shut loudly behind her. But her brief spurt of defiance soon drained away as she took her first good look at the garment she had so hastily seized from her chest of drawers. Oh, lord! This thin, flimsy nightgown was likely to be no better than the short towel she was wearing.

In fact, she told herself gloomily a few moments later, it was a good deal worse! Grimacing with dismay, and unable to avoid the sight of herself in the mirrors which lined the room, she desperately tried to tug the edges of the minuscule bodice closer together. Attempting to hide the deep creamy cleft between her breasts, Tiffany soon realised that she had another, major problem.

A quick glance in the mirrored wall behind her confirmed her worst suspicions: the diaphanous black nightgown was practically transparent! And, while Maxine might well have fancied herself in this erotic-looking négligé, Tiffany could only hope and pray that a thunderbolt would strike down the dreadful man, who was so calmly making himself at home in the bedroom next door.

Unfortunately, she knew that her prayers had no chance of being answered. After giving the thin, shoelace straps of the garment another hopeless tug upwards, she tried to brace herself for the forth-coming ordeal.

'I'm not coming out of here—not unless you promise to close your eyes!' Tiffany announced tre-mulously as she opened the door a crack, only her head visible as she glared across the bedroom at the man who was, quite maddeningly, coolly reading one of the books from her bedside table.

'I mean it!' she added tersely, her embarrassment quickly turning to anger as Zarco gave a short bark of sardonic laughter. 'If you don't close your eyes—and stop laughing—I shall stay in here. All night, if need be!'

Zarco shook his head and gave a heavy, impatient sigh. 'This is clearly quite ridiculous. Especially since I am a married man, and well used to the sight of my wife in a négligé.'

'Not *this* wife, you're not!' Tiffany snapped, before making good her threat and firmly closing the door.

She wasn't really going to stay in here all night, she consoled herself as she leant wearily back against the wooden panels of the small door. However, she was at least safe in here for the time being. A comforting thought, which was swiftly dispelled a moment later when the door was violently thrown open, the force of the blow propelling her across the room.

'Ouch . . . !' she moaned, wincing as she rubbed the shin-bone of her leg where it had banged against the edge of the bath. 'There was no need to barge in here like that,' she grumbled, turning to face the man whose tall figure filled the doorway.

'There was every need,' he grated forcefully. 'I want you out of here—*right now*!'

After a swift glance at his stern, angry expression, and the rigid stance of his tense body, Tiffany quickly decided there was little point in arguing any further. Raising her chin defiantly, she stalked past him, before throwing her dignity to the wind as she dashed across the room, quickly scrambling beneath the covers of the large four-poster bed.

'I have had quite enough of this nonsense!' Zarco stated flatly, advancing slowly across the room towards her. 'I have said I wish to talk to you—and that is exactly what I intend to do.'

He pulled the chair closer to the bed, before sitting down and regarding her with a hard, determined expression in his dark eyes.

Tiffany, anxious to cover as much of her semi-naked flesh as possible, nervously raised the sheet to her chin, inching as far back against the pillows as possible.

'Have I made myself clear?' he demanded, and, when she responded with an apprehensive nod, some of the rigid stiffness seemed to drain out of his long body.

'Very well,' he continued, leaning back in the comfortable chair. 'Earlier this evening you accused me of not only being blind—but also of not being able to admit that I might have made a mistake. And so, after giving the matter some considerable thought, I am prepared to listen to what you have to say.'

'And about time too!' she muttered under her breath.

Zarco blandly ignored her interruption. 'Let us assume, just for the moment, that you are who you say you are: that you are "Tiffany Harris". If so, I think that you should start by telling me everything you can remember about yourself.'

Tiffany gave a helpless shrug. 'Well, I'll try to do my best . . . but I'm still having difficulty remembering *exact* dates and times,' she said, before staring down fixedly at the sheet as she tried to concentrate on the problem. This was clearly her best opportunity to try and open Zarco's eyes to the fact that she *wasn't* Maxine—and she must try to recall every single scrap of helpful information which had been slowly floating back into her mind during the past few days.

Slowly and hesitantly, she began to describe her life with the great-aunts who had brought her up following the death of her parents, Martin and Harriette Kendall. 'I expect I was a bit of a pain in the neck,' she admitted with a slight, rueful smile. 'But I missed my father and mother so much, and my life in that grim Victorian house was so awful that it's no wonder I took the first opportunity to run away from home!'

She was surprised to find that Zarco was surprisingly understanding when she confessed that there were still some large gaps in her life which she hadn't been able to fill. She could remember her runaway wedding to Brian Harris—and the fact that he was a not very successful professional tennis player.

'It's crazy, really.' She brushed a distracted hand through her short, wavy gold hair. 'I could draw you a complete layout of the courts at Wimbledon, Flushing Meadow and Forest Lawn. But . . . but I don't . . . I can't remember what's happened to Brian.' She gazed at Zarco in distress.

'Ah, yes—the elusive Brian Harris,' he drawled smoothly. 'Were you happy with your husband?'

Unfortunately, that was one part of her life which she could remember only too well. 'No, I...' She faltered, bitterly aware of a deep flush rising over her pale cheeks.

'Are you trying to say that you weren't happy—or that you cannot remember?' Zarco enquired drily.

Tiffany glared at him. Why couldn't the damned man mind his own business? 'No, I wasn't happy,' she snapped. 'And that's all I'm prepared to say on the subject!'

'Very well,' he murmured coolly. 'Leaving aside your unhappy marriage, what else can you remember about this life of yours?'

'Not much,' she admitted ruefully. 'I think...I think I remember packing our suitcases, and Brian telling me to hurry up, because we were going to be late for the flight to London, and...' Tiffany paused, closing her eyes as she tried to concentrate very hard on the faint thread of remembered sound. 'And...we *had* to catch the flight, to make our connection with the plane to...to Faro. Yes—*that's it*! Brian was being hired by a tennis club in the Algarve. That's in Portugal, isn't it?' she asked with a frown.

'Indeed it is,' Zarco drawled slowly. 'And how long ago was this trip to the Algarve?'

Tiffany shrugged. 'I don't feel that it was very long ago...but I really can't be sure about that,' she confessed unhappily.

Seeing that the girl was obviously distressed, Zarco decided to change the subject. 'We seem to have a brief outline of your life. However, I don't think I have asked how old you are.'

'Yes, well—that's one thing I *am* fairly sure about,' she told him, her spirits lifting at being able to be positive about one aspect of her life, at least. 'My birthday is on September the sixth. And I *know* that I am not yet twenty-five, because on my twenty-fifth birthday I'm due to inherit a considerable amount of money from a trust fund set up by my parents. I know that I haven't yet had the money, so I think I must be only about twenty-three or twenty-four years of age. No wonder I never felt that I was Maxine's age of twenty-seven—I knew I couldn't be *that* old!'

Zarco's shoulders shook with amusement. 'If twenty-seven is old, how do you think *I* feel at the ripe old age of thirty-eight?'

'Goodness—you don't look that ancient!' she exclaimed without thinking, before his snort of dry, cynical laughter made her realise that she might have put her foot in it. 'Oh—er—I didn't mean to be rude, or...'

'On the contrary—I rather think that I'm flattered by your reaction!' he said, giving her such a warm and infectious grin that she was amazed to find herself smiling tentatively back at him. And, since he appeared to be in a better mood, maybe this was the perfect moment for her to ask the sixty-four-thousand-dollar question.

'Have I... have I managed to convince you that I really am Tiffany Harris?' she asked him nervously, her shoulders drooping in dejection and despair as he gave a slight shake of his dark head.

'No, not one hundred per cent,' he told her quietly. 'You see, I have been married for some years to a woman whom I *know* to be a cheat and a liar. A very plausible and clever woman, who would be quite capable not only of convincing Harley Street specialists that she had completely lost her memory, but also able to concoct a completely new life for herself, such as you have just described.'

Zarco rose, pushing away the chair as he began to pace up and down the room. 'So, although I would like to accept what you say, believe me, I have been given good reasons in the past to be very cautious,' he added grimly.

Tiffany gave a heavy sigh. 'I believe you,' she muttered glumly. 'But what I *can't* understand is why you don't instinctively know that I'm not Maxine? I mean...' She frowned and shook her head as she tried to find the words. 'There's always more to someone than a...a physical presence, if you see what I mean? I know that I'm not expressing this very well, but if I was to see my parents again—even after all these years, and even if they looked completely different— I'm sure I would immediately recognise their individual personalities.'

'My wife and I lived very separate lives,' Zarco told her dismissively.

Tiffany sighed. 'You simply don't seem to understand,' she muttered. 'For instance, I *know* that I've never met you before. And that's not just because I don't recognise you—but also because the essential part of you, the personal aura you carry about with you, is totally unfamiliar. Surely you must see what I mean?' she added helplessly. 'Or is it that you are so fed up with Maxine, both for stealing your jewels and because you actively disliked her, that you can't see beyond the end of your nose?'

Zarco frowned as her voice rose in exasperation. 'Of course I understand what you are trying to say. But what *you* seem to fail to understand is the plain fact that every time I look at you—I see my wife!'

'Yes, I know,' she murmured gloomily. 'How on earth did you come to marry the awful woman in the first place?'

'It's a long story,' he told her curtly. 'And, unfortunately, not one which reflects any credit on myself.'

Tiffany gazed up at the man who had come to a halt beside the bed, and who was clearly buried in his own dark thoughts as he leaned against the carved bedpost. Watching as he pushed a hand through his dark hair, ruffling its normally sleek surface, and the heavy half-closed eyelids beneath which he was clearly retracing uncomfortable memories of his past, she was suddenly swept by a strong tide of deep compassion and sympathy for the unhappy man.

Totally confounded by such an unexpectedly strong emotional response towards a man whom she disliked and feared, she couldn't help giving a small gasp. The slight sound broke into his abstracted thoughts and he turned, his eyes narrowing thoughtfully as he viewed the unguarded expression on her face.

She could feel a deep flush spreading over her skin—an extraordinary sensation of white heat surging through her body. The room seemed to be shrinking about them, their two still figures caught in a time-warp, one in which she felt increasingly weak and light-headed. The strained silence seemed to last forever—beating loudly on her eardrums as her mind was filled with the disturbing sensual memories of the times when she'd found herself clasped in his arms.

As he slowly moved over to sit down on the bed beside her nervous, trembling figure, her heart began to pound like a heavy drum. The thudding beat against her ribs produced a swift surge of adrenalin throughout her body, leaving her breathless as though she'd just been running a race.

Her mouth was dry with fear and tension and, as she moistened her lips with her tongue, he seemed to stiffen, his low, tersely muttered oath cutting into the claustrophobic and oppressive silence.

She was unable to tear her eyes away from his hypnotic gaze, aware only of the strong, tanned column of his throat, the high angular cheekbones and the cruel, sensual curve of his mouth.

'I wonder why you appear to be so afraid of me?' he murmured slowly. 'Or, is it yourself—and your own emotions—of which you are frightened . . . ?'

'I . . . I'm not frightened of . . . of anything,' she managed to gasp, so acutely aware of him that it was almost a physical agony. Why did this man have the power to upset and disturb her so easily?

Her brain a morass of chaotic thoughts and feelings, she was still gazing blindly up at him when she felt his warm hand touch her cheek, her body quivering and shaking almost uncontrollably in reply to the unmistakable darkening gleam in his eyes.

'No. . . please!' she gasped as she felt his hand moving down her neck, his fingers slowly trailing over the fine bones and soft skin of her bare shoulders, lightly brushing aside the thin strap of her nightgown. 'Zarco—no . . . !'

'I have told you before that you have a beautiful body,' he murmured, ignoring her strangled gasps of protest as he swept aside the other strap before impatiently pulling down her gown and the useless barrier of the sheet to cup his hands around her quivering flesh.

Tiffany knew she must stop him—right now! But when his tanned fingers moved enticingly over the hardening tips of her breasts she was unable to withstand the fiery excitement zigzagging through her body as he lowered his dark head, his mouth closing possessively over one enlarged, swollen nipple.

'You may tell me no—but your body is saying *yes!*' he breathed huskily against her skin, before his warm lips trailed a scorching path over her quivering flesh towards her other breast.

His fingers slipped down over her skin towards her waist, and she shivered convulsively, her throat dry and parched with the deep need and excitement she could feel raging within her. She had a crazy desire to slide her fingers through the thick, ruffled darkness of his hair, to clasp his head against her throbbing breasts, her trembling hands aching to caress the strong male contours of his body. Embarrassment, shame and fear mingled together into a tight knot in her stomach as she desperately tried to control her wild emotions, which seemed to be spinning dizzily out of control.

She must do something! It was sheer madness to allow him to continue to arouse her in this way! Tiffany screamed silently at her weak body. But her soft, yielding flesh resolutely refused to heed the warning. She was only aware of the driving need to surrender to the passionate desire racing through her veins, her body melting helplessly beneath the dizzy, spiralling excitement which she had never known before.

'Your skin has the silky softness of velvet,' he murmured against her flesh, his mouth trailing a hot, scorching path down to her navel. Heat flared and burned through her veins. Half of her distraught and bewildered mind wanted to escape from this delicious torture, to flee as far away from him as she possibly could. And yet...the other half of her confused brain was strongly urging her towards an even closer intimacy; she felt a craving need and yearning to cast aside all her instinctive inhibitions and respond to such a wealth of rich, sensual delight.

Helpless beneath the masterly sureness of his touch, the breath catching in her throat as she felt his hands moving slowly down over her trembling thighs and the wet, moist caresses of his mouth and tongue, she gave a small unhappy moan as he slowly raised his head and stared down into her dazed eyes.

'It is obvious that you want me,' he stated flatly.

'No!' she cried, knowing that, despite her instinctive denial, he spoke nothing but the truth. She did want to touch Zarco as freely and openly as he was touching her, to taste the warm masculine scent of his skin, and to feel his hard, strong flesh come alive beneath her fingers.

'Don't try to fool yourself,' he told her roughly, his lips twisting as he gazed bleakly down at her flushed, naked body—the body that was obviously crying out for his touch, her nipples aching for the erotic, moist caress of his mouth and tongue.

'But, enticing as I may find you, I have no intention of being so foolish as to fall for this honey trap,' he added grimly. 'Until I am totally certain of who or what you are, I shall have to say ''thanks—but no, thanks!'''

Completely dazed, and quite unable to believe that this was happening to her, Tiffany lay paralysed as he slowly rose to his feet. With a bitter, mocking expression he bent down to lightly toss the sheet over her nakedness, before turning to walk silently out of the room.

Later, lying alone in the darkness, Tiffany couldn't believe that she had ever felt such depths of humiliation, or such wretched unhappiness, as she did at this moment. Turning to bury her face in the soft pillows, there seemed nothing she could do to prevent herself from giving way to a storm of tears, her slender body convulsed by sobs of total desolation.

CHAPTER SIX

As THE Aston Martin scorched down the motorway, Tiffany leaned back in her comfortable soft leather seat. The increasingly claustrophobic, oppressive silence within the vehicle was only escalating the strain felt by her tense, nervous body.

Zarco had remained totally silent so far, guiding the powerful car through the heavy traffic with consummate skill. She was vibrantly aware of the long fingers firmly grasping the steering-wheel, and the liberal sprinkling of black hair on his hard, muscular tanned arms beneath the short-sleeved silk shirt.

Stealing a fleeting glance through her eyelashes at his stern profile, the lines and planes of his handsome features highlighted by the strong sunlight flooding into the car, Tiffany clasped her hands tightly together. She must…she simply *must* try to stamp out this sick longing—a totally crazy urge to be clasped once again to his hard male chest—to rest her head against those strong shoulders. A small moan involuntarily broke from her lips, and she quickly tried to mask it with a cough.

'Are you feeling all right?' Zarco quickly turned his head to glance at the girl sitting so silently beside him. 'Would you care to listen to some music?'

She gave a slight shrug of her shoulders, turning her head to stare out of the car at the passing traffic, praying that he wouldn't notice the quick, hectic flush which she could feel sweeping over her face.

'Yes, maybe some music would be a good idea,' she muttered, trying to control the unnaturally husky, breathless tone in her voice.

A moment later, Tiffany found herself dearly wishing that she'd kept silent. Goodness knows what had prompted him to select this particular cassette. But, as the authentic strains of the Portuguese *Fado* singer filled the small space within the vehicle, the sad and melancholic tones of the haunting music reflected the desolation in her own heart.

The last few days seemed to have been quite the longest of her life. Tiffany was sure that she'd never felt quite so miserable. It was as though she inhabited a wretchedly lonely, alien planet, and nothing could seem to lift the heavy weight of her despair. Especially when it became obvious that Zarco had been deliberately avoiding her—almost as if she had some dreadful, infectious disease.

After the traumatic scene in her bedroom, she had slept fitfully, tossing and turning in the night as her weary mind and body were racked by painful dreams. Awaking the next morning, it took her a few moments to become aware of her surroundings, to realise that what she had imagined to be a fearful nightmare was an all too true reality. She was far too agitated to remain in bed, but it wasn't until she was gazing at her pale, listless face in the bathroom mirror that Tiffany suddenly realised part of her memory had returned.

It was…it was quite extraordinary and almost weird to discover how easily she could recall all the missing details of her life with Brian. As if, in some mysterious and strange manner, Zarco's lovemaking last night had unlocked part of her brain. Even if she had wanted to, there was nothing she could do to prevent

her mind being filled with the flickering images of her
marriage—up to and including Brian's tragic death.

Despite feeling totally washed out and listless after
her sleepless night, and also hideously embarrassed
at having to face Zarco so soon after his cruel, almost
sadistic behaviour of the previous evening, she knew
she had no choice. She must give him all the details
of her past life which she had now recalled. Because,
with this fresh information to corroborate her story,
he could easily check out and confirm the details for
himself.

Hurriedly getting dressed, Tiffany nervously
checked her appearance in the mirror. Unfortunately,
the aspirins she'd taken for the headache that throbbed
and pounded in her head didn't seem to be working
at all. She was still feeling like death warmed up, and
there was nothing she could do to hide the dark circles
beneath her shadowy blue eyes. However, after
spending some time sorting through Maxine dos
Santos's elaborate, expensive clothes, she had
managed to find a simple sleeveless cotton blouse and
matching blue skirt, in which she did at least feel
reasonably comfortable.

Moving apprehensively through the empty house,
she eventually tracked Zarco down in the kitchen,
having a few words with Amy Long who'd just returned from visiting her married daughter in Oxford.

'I've been trying to find you,' she told him breathlessly. 'I . . . I've just remembered a whole lot more
about Brian, and——'

'Can't you see that I'm busy talking to Mrs Long?'
he demanded, lifting one dark brow as if astonished
that she should have the temerity to interrupt his conversation. 'I will see you in the library in half an hour,'
he added, his dark eyes sweeping scathingly over her

nervous figure as he gave a brief, dismissive flick of his fingers before turning back to continue his conversation.

Furious at being treated as though she were something nasty that the cat had just dragged in, Tiffany nevertheless found herself obeying his terse instructions. Too much had happened to her lately—too many trials and tribulations—for her to be able to throw off her present downcast, forlorn state of mind. After she had trailed dejectedly into the library, it had seemed as though she'd been waiting for ages before Zarco condescended to join her.

'What is it you wish to say to me?' he demanded in a cold, hard voice as he entered the room, barely giving her a glance as he strode towards the large leather-topped mahogany desk in a far corner beneath the large mullioned windows. 'I am very busy— and have no time to waste on any female nonsense!'

Tiffany flushed at the harsh sarcasm in his voice. 'I . . . I have no intention of wasting your precious time!' she protested huskily, despising herself for still being so helplessly drawn towards this hateful man. 'I only wanted to tell you that, when I woke up this morning, I discovered that I could remember all about my life with my husband, Brian.'

'How convenient!' he sneered, not bothering to turn around as he sat down at the desk and pulled a file towards him. 'Am I supposed to congratulate you?'

She frowned in puzzlement. 'For what?'

'For realising that your story had as many holes as a leaky sieve!' He gave a harsh, bleak laugh. 'I imagine that you must have spent most of the night trying to remedy the damage, and in attempting to fill the gaps in your so-called past life.'

'That's not true!' she gasped.

'No...?'

'*No*! I promise you that what I am saying is the *truth*!' she insisted, her face paling beneath the scorn in those glittering dark eyes. 'I can now remember everything. All about my husband drinking too much, and his terrible car crash. Brian was in a coma for almost a year before he...he died without regaining consciousness. I really *am* telling the truth,' she assured the man continuing to sit with his back to her, apparently absorbed in the papers in front of him.

'I honestly don't know why I haven't recalled everything until now,' she continued in the face of his stony silence. 'Brian was in the hospital for such a long time that they're bound to have records to support what I say. And *that's* why I was in Lisbon,' she added, moving hesitantly across the carpet towards him. 'I had to stay down in the Algarve for some time, to earn enough money to pay for my plane fare back to England. And I only broke my journey in Lisbon, just to see something of the old city before going on to England.'

'A likely tale!'

Tiffany gazed at him, speechless for a moment. Did this man never give up? Was it totally impossible for him to accept that he could have been wrong?

'It's *not* a tale. I'm telling you the truth!' she reiterated firmly. 'And if I was going to tell a lie, I'd make up a better one than what happened when I arrived in Lisbon, because I was stupid enough not to know that it was a national holiday, and that it would be practically impossible to find anywhere to stay. I do remember travelling into the city in a taxi, but...I can't remember any more,' she added with a helpless shrug. 'Surely you must believe me?' she pleaded.

'Why should I?' he grated in a cold, hard voice as he turned slowly to face her. 'If you imagine that by attempting to entice me with your body you have succeeded in persuading me that you are not my wife, you are *very* much mistaken.'

Tiffany gasped, flinching under the cruel whiplash of his caustic words. 'I didn't...'

He gave a harsh, humourless laugh. 'I can assure you that I am not to be seduced from the truth quite so easily!'

'That's a rotten thing to say! It wasn't *me* who was doing the seducing last night!' Her voice wobbled dangerously as she fought to control the tears which were threatening to fall at any minute. 'I may have been married, but no one has ever...ever touched me like that before. And as an experienced man of the world, you ought to know that!' she sobbed, before fleeing out of the room, her eyes blind with tears.

And that was the last that Tiffany had seen of Zarco for the next three days.

It was unusually hot for the time of year, and she'd been plagued by tension headaches, which had grown increasingly severe as each day passed. There seemed nothing she could do to prevent herself from constantly thinking about the totally disastrous, cataclysmic scene in her bedroom, or her pathetically helpless response to Zarco's cynical lovemaking. How could he have used and abused her in such a way? Surely he must know, in his heart of hearts, that she *wasn't* his wife Maxine?

However, Zarco had provided no clue to his savage treatment of her. Mostly because she had hardly seen him during the last few days, she reminded herself bitterly, recalling how he had locked himself away in the library. There, with a battery of modern telecommunication aids at his disposal, he had apparently been immersed in conducting his world-wide business affairs. He'd even had all his meals in the solitary grandeur of the book-lined room, with its sombre decoration of dark red velvet curtains and the muted glow of priceless Persian carpets.

Nothing had occurred to interrupt her desperately lonely, melancholy existence. Even Amy Long—undoubtedly under the influence of her employer—had reverted from her brief friendship to a cautious and guarded manner, making it clear that Tiffany was no longer welcome in her kitchen. In fact, it wasn't until the unexpected appearance of Ralph Pargeter, after breakfast this morning, that she'd had any hope of escaping from her prison at Norton Manor.

The tall, fair-haired man, who had swept up the drive in a black Porsche, had done much to restore her damaged self-esteem. Announcing that he was sorry not to have called to see her before now, but his mother had only just contacted him on his return from holiday, Ralph Pargeter had proved to be a charming man.

'I can't tell you how glad I am that my mama asked me to call,' he grinned as she led him into the large drawing-room. 'I wonder why she never told me what a stunningly pretty girl you are?'

'Probably because I was looking simply ghastly in the hospital!' Tiffany told him with a smile before asking Amy Long, who was hovering in the doorway, if she would provide a pot of coffee for their visitor.

'I was so grateful for all the help and support your mother gave me,' she told Ralph, as he came over to sit down on the sofa beside her. 'I was nearly going mad, trying to prove that I wasn't the wife of the man who owns this house.' She shrugged unhappily. 'I still haven't succeeded, of course, but I can't tell you what it meant to have someone actually *believe* what I said!'

'Have you managed to remember any more of your past life, since leaving Lisbon?' he asked.

'Yes, I have—practically everything. But it doesn't seem to have done me much good,' she sighed, her blue eyes shadowed with the pain and misery of the past few days.

Explaining to this friendly and handsome young man what she could recall of her past life, Tiffany told him how she still hadn't managed to remember what had happened after she'd arrived in Lisbon. 'And I don't seem to have found any way in which I can definitely prove that I'm not that awful woman Maxine dos Santos.'

'Well, I wouldn't worry about that,' Ralph told her breezily. 'By far the easiest option is for you to prove that you really *are* Tiffany Harris, right? And that's easy! All you have to do, is to toddle along to St Catherine's House.'

'Where...?' she was asking with a frown when Amy Long returned with a tray, containing a silver coffee-pot and some cups and saucers. Noting the older woman's stiff figure, rigid with disapproval, Tiffany was surprised when the housekeeper announced that Zarco was having a few words with the head gardener, but would be returning to the house shortly.

'I say—she looks a bit of an old dragon!' Ralph exclaimed when Amy, after giving him a freezing glance, had stalked stiffly out of the room. 'Are you finding life here a bit grim?'

Tiffany gave a slight shrug of her shoulders. 'It's not easy,' she admitted, surprised to find herself reluctant to blacken Zarco's character. 'And Amy has been very kind, really. It's just that she, and everyone

else who works in this house, is very much in awe of
my so-called husband. Actually...' She gave a nervous
giggle. 'It's just occurred to me—Amy probably thinks
that you're my "fancy man"!'

'Your *what*...?' Ralph looked at her in astonishment for a moment, before Tiffany quickly put him
in the picture regarding both Maxine's character, and
the housekeeper's suspicions about the other woman's
boyfriend.

Ralph laughed. 'Oh, I see—she thinks it's a case
of history repeating itself, does she? Well...' He
grinned wolfishly at the beautiful girl sitting beside
him. 'I'd be happy to join the list of *your* admirers!'

Tiffany blushed. Ralph was obviously a very nice,
kind man. However, she'd never been one of those
people who enjoyed carrying on a light flirtation—
and she certainly didn't intend to start doing so now.

'Thank you for the compliment,' she muttered,
hiding her embarrassment as she busied herself with
pouring him a cup of coffee. 'If we could—er—return
to what you were saying, before Amy came in...?'

'Oh, yes—I was telling you about St Catherine's
House, wasn't I?' Ralph said, taking both his cup of
coffee, and his rejection by the beautiful girl, with
equal aplomb. 'St Catherine's House in Kingsway,
London, is where they keep all the records for births,
marriages and deaths. So, if you can remember your
own birthday or when you were born, and the date
of your marriage, you shouldn't have any trouble in
being able to prove who you are.'

'Really...?'

Ralph nodded. 'And driving over here, today, I had
one or two other ideas. For instance: it would be a
real help if you can remember the name and address
of a doctor who might have known you. And the real

cruncher—if you'll forgive the pun!—is if you can recall the name of your dentist. I don't know how long you've been abroad, but if you had your teeth seen to before you left this country the person you saw is very likely still to have your dental records.'

Tiffany's blue eyes sparkled. 'You are clever—that's a really brilliant idea!'

Ralph smiled, clearly pleased with himself for having come up with some helpful solutions to the girl's problem. 'I read somewhere that teeth are like fingerprints—because, apparently, no two person's teeth are exactly the same,' he told her. 'So, with your birth and marriage certificates, plus a doctor and dentist's verification, it will be easy to prove *exactly* who you are.'

'That's terrific!' she exclaimed, her eyes glowing with relief at the thought of at last being able to do something positive. 'So what you're saying is that I should forget the dreadful mistake everyone has made about Maxine? That I should just concentrate on establishing my own background?'

Ralph nodded. 'Absolutely! After all, once you've definitely proved that you're Tiffany Harris, it's going to be up to your "husband" to look elsewhere for his errant wife. And you...' Ralph leaned forward, putting a friendly arm around her shoulders '...*you* can just snap your fingers at Zarco dos Santos!'

'Do I hear my name being mentioned?'

The deep voice from the doorway behind them startled both Ralph and Tiffany.

'Enter the Demon King!' Ralph muttered under his breath, scrambling to his feet as Zarco strode into the room.

Tiffany, who'd felt a hysterical bubble of nervous laughter rising in her throat at Ralph's description—

Zarco *did* seem to carry around with him a frightening aura of brimstone and sulphur!—swallowed hard as she was subjected to a swift, crushing glance from Zarco's cold dark eyes.

'I don't believe I've had the pleasure of meeting you before?' he drawled, turning to smile blandly at the younger man.

'No. My mother, Mrs Emily Pargeter, asked me to call and see your wife,' Ralph told him quickly. 'My mother regularly visits patients at the hospital, in Lisbon, and...'

'Ah, yes. Who could forget Mrs Pargeter? An indomitable old lady! I trust she is well?' Zarco enquired smoothly.

As Zarco and Ralph continued their somewhat over-polite conversation, Tiffany was struck by the contrast between the two men. Ralph, who initially had appeared to be a confident, tall and handsome man, now seemed to be somehow insignificant when compared to the much taller, more dominant figure of Zarco, whose dark good looks completely eclipsed the pale, English colouring of the younger man.

'So, you're a foreign exchange dealer, are you? And how is business these days?' Zarco was asking in a clearly bored tone of voice, as Tiffany realised that she had been so absorbed in her thoughts that she'd missed some of their conversation.

'Oh, it's not too bad. It comes and goes,' Ralph told him cheerfully, obviously not too worried about losing his wealthy lifestyle.

Zarco gave him a bland, chilly smile. 'Well, you have come—but I'm afraid that we must go,' he drawled, smoothly turning to take hold of Tiffany's hand, which was lying on the arm of the sofa, and drawing her quickly to her feet. 'My wife and I are due to visit my son's school today, and I'm afraid that we have to leave straight away.'

Tiffany turned to look at him in astonishment. 'I don't remember you saying anything about...' she began, faltering as she felt his fingers biting like steel talons into the soft flesh of her arm.

'My dear wife has this small problem with her memory,' Zarco murmured sardonically to Ralph, still keeping a firm grip on her slim, trembling figure. 'So, if you will forgive us...'

'Oh, yes—of course. I only called in for a few minutes,' Ralph muttered, clearly caught between his years of upbringing as a polite Englishman, and the desire not to leave this obviously frightened girl alone; especially not in the threatening clutches of such an ominous-looking foreigner.

However, his ingrained national characteristics won the day. And, after giving Tiffany a faint hollow smile, he allowed himself to be issued out of the house by Zarco.

'I'm not having that spineless idiot calling here again!' Zarco growled as he returned to the sitting-room, where she had nervously collapsed down into a chair. 'If that silly young wimp thinks that he can just turn up, and flirt with my wife, he's *very* much mistaken!'

'Ralph wasn't doing anything of the sort!' she protested.

He gave a harsh, sardonic snort of laughter. 'Oh, no? If he was just making a neighbourly call, maybe you can tell me why his arm was around your shoulder?' he ground out angrily.

'He was being friendly and...and helpful, that's all!' she exclaimed helplessly, her cheeks flushing as Zarco gave another cynical bark of mirthless laughter.

Tiffany bit back the angry, bitter retort that hovered on her tongue, knowing that anything she had to say would only give him the opportunity to make yet another blistering comment about Emily's son.

There was no way he was going to believe her, she realised. Equally, there was no way she could tell him about Ralph's ideas to prove her identity. Any mention of her plans to obtain copies of her own birth and marriage certificates would merely give this dangerous man advance warning of her intentions. And besides, why should she have to explain herself, when she'd clearly been doing nothing wrong?

'Hurry up—we haven't much time,' Zarco's voice broke into her distracted thoughts. When she gazed at him in bewilderment, he added impatiently, 'We are going to see Carlos at his school—remember?'

'But I thought that was just an excuse you made, to get rid of Ralph Pargeter...?'

Zarco lifted one dark, quizzical eyebrow. 'What an extraordinary idea. I wonder why you should think that?' he drawled coolly.

Tiffany wondered why, too. And, since those had been the last words he'd spoken to her, other than insisting that they must leave immediately, she had spent most of the journey so far trying to work out what was going on. Zarco had acted towards Ralph in a thoroughly peculiar manner. Just like a dog with a bone. In fact, if it weren't too ridiculous, she might think that he'd been behaving like a jealous husband!

Carlos dos Santos was proving to be an amusing young boy, and very different from what Tiffany had imagined.

'I say, Dad—this is absolutely terrific!' the boy mumbled, happily chomping his way through a third slice of Amy Long's Black Forest gâteau.

Tiffany, not used to the ravenous appetite of young boys, had watched with fascination and increasing awe as Zarco's son swiftly demolished most of the contents of a large, well stocked picnic basket. Surely, it wasn't possible for the child's thin frame to be able to absorb *quite* so many chicken drumsticks and cold sausages, as well as a mountain of ham sandwiches and four packets of crisps? Her sapphire-blue eyes had grown round with astonishment as he proceeded to tuck into the chocolate gâteau, while emptying at least three cans of fizzy orange!

'I think you've probably had sufficient, Carlos,' Zarco said at last, when even he, who must have been used to this boy's gargantuan appetite, clearly felt his son had eaten quite enough.

'For heaven's sake, Dad!' the boy grimaced, looking quickly over his shoulder to see if any of the other picnickers in the school grounds could hear what they were saying. '*Please* don't call me Carlos. All the other fellows call me Charlie—and I *much* prefer it,' he added, gazing anxiously at his father.

As Zarco frowned with irritation, Tiffany—who had immediately understood why his son should wish to change his name—instinctively found herself intervening on the boy's behalf.

'I know what you mean, Charlie,' she told him ruefully, being careful not to look in Zarco's direction. 'My full name is Tiffany Imogen Catherine Kendall, and until I was about fourteen years old everyone at school called me ''Tick'' or ''Tick-Tock''. I hated it—especially when the other girls used to call out, ''Here comes Tick-Tock.'' I know it doesn't sound very bad,' she told Zarco hesitantly. 'But children can be very cruel, and it made my life an absolute misery.'

Charlie nodded vigorously in support. 'She—er—she's right, Dad,' the boy muttered, obviously confused as to what to call this woman, who was claiming that she wasn't his dreaded stepmother, Maxine dos Santos. 'It's just...well, I don't want to be different from the other boys, if you see what I mean?'

To Tiffany's complete surprise, Zarco responded by giving his son a warm smile, and holding up his hands in mock surrender. 'Very well—Charlie it shall be from now on. After all,' he added with a slight laugh, 'with the two of you in complete agreement, who am I to disagree?'

Zarco dos Santos—*that's who*! Tiffany thought grimly, still having considerable difficulty in accepting that this warm, humorous and relaxed man could be the same hard, menacing personality who'd so dominated her life over the past few weeks.

From the first moment they had arrived at Charlie's boarding-school, Tiffany had been struck by not only the obvious pride Zarco took in his son, but also his deep love and concern for the motherless boy. Charlie, too, clearly adored his father, greeting his arrival for the school's sports day with a wide, beaming smile. And although the young boy clearly had severe reservations, if not an active dislike of his stepmother, the few words he had addressed to her had been scrupulously polite. It wasn't until they had begun the picnic, under the shade of some old oak trees surrounding the cricket pitch, that Charlie had gradually become more relaxed towards her. And now, as Tiffany began to clear up the remnants of their picnic, she was surprised to hear Zarco suggest that, as he needed to have a few words with the headmaster, maybe Charlie would like to show her around the school?

'Maybe he would prefer to join his friends?' she told Zarco quickly, almost sure that the last thing Charlie wanted was to be lumbered with a step-mother. However, she was pleasantly surprised when the boy merely gave a casual nod, and agreed to his father's suggestion.

'This is my classroom,' Carlos told her some time later as they reached the end of the conducted tour. 'Are you all right?' he added, looking with concern at the woman as she leaned against the wall, ob-viously buried deep in thought.

'Yes, I'm fine.' Tiffany gave herself a mental shake. 'It's just…I'm finding it quite extraordinary how little schools have changed since my day. There's the same dusty smell of the chalk used on blackboards—and I bet if I opened your desk I would find it was in a thorough mess!' she grinned.

Charlie laughed. 'You're right!' he said, going to a small desk in the front row. Lifting the lid, he grinned sheepishly down at the clutter and confusion of exercise books, pens and pencils—and what looked suspiciously like a small jar of frog-spawn!

'You seem to be doing rather well in most of your subjects,' Tiffany said, studying a chart on the wall. 'Although it looks as though you've got problems with arithmetic.'

'Yes,' the boy sighed heavily. 'Dad's so clever at maths, but I seem to be absolutely hopeless.'

'When I was your age, I used to be quite good at the subject. Would you like to show me what you are doing at the moment? Maybe I could give you some help?' she offered hesitantly.

Charlie looked at her dubiously for a moment, before giving a slight shrug of his young shoulders. 'I don't suppose it will be much use. Especially since we've got a test tomorrow,' he told her, giving another sigh of despondency as he removed an exercise book from his desk . . .

'So, if I put this here, and that there . . . ? Hey—*it works*!' Charlie exclaimed some time later, giving her a smile that was so like his father's that Tiffany could almost feel her heart turn over.

'I can show you some more maths tricks, if you like?'

'I certainly *would*!' Charlie grinned, turning his head as Zarco entered the empty classroom.

'Ah, there you are,' he said as the boy scrambled to his feet and dashed across the room.

'She's a real whizzo genius at maths, Dad! I bet Old Barney will drop dead with shock when he sees how easily I can do those beastly sums!'

Zarco smiled fondly down at the boy. 'If you are referring to your teacher, Mr Barnard, I imagine that he probably will,' he told his son drily. 'I've just been hearing about your problems with mathematics.'

'Not any more!' Charlie told him gleefully, missing the hard, razor-sharp glance his father cast at Tiffany before following the boy out of the classroom.

For the rest of the afternoon, while watching the various games and races—and applauding Charlie, who was thrilled with himself for having come second in the one-hundred-metres race—Tiffany was aware of Zarco occasionally turning his dark, narrowed gaze in her direction. It was as if, like his son, he too was having difficulty in getting his sums right.

However, surrounded as they were by a milling crowd of parents, vigorously and noisily encouraging their sons during the various sports events, there was no opportunity for him to speak privately to her. A fact which, after their tense, stressful journey to the school, helped to soothe her battered spirits. Sitting quietly in the dappled shade of the trees surrounding the field, Tiffany was able, for almost the first time that day, to think about what Ralph Pargeter had said.

Although she was deeply grateful to Emily's son for suggesting several excellent, practical ways in which she could prove her identity, there were still some hard and tough facts of life which she had to overcome. If and when she managed to convince Zarco that he had indeed made a great mistake, what on earth was she going to do next?

Zarco *might* be kind enough to lend her some money, enabling her to rent a very small flat in London while she looked for a job—but she couldn't count on his being that generous, could she? Zarco was many things—but 'kind' or 'generous' weren't qualities which sprang instantly to mind when thinking of his hard, tough personality. Indeed, it was far more likely that he would be furious and extremely unhelpful! After all, once she'd proved that he *had* made a grave error, such proof was also going to make him look a complete fool. A man who didn't even know his own wife was likely to be an object of derision to his friends and acquaintances. In fact, the thought of Zarco's likely reaction in those circumstances was enough to make her shudder and tremble with fear.

However, that was only the first of her problems. It was almost overwhelmingly daunting to realise that she possessed absolutely *nothing* of her previous life. Why, even the wedding-ring she was wearing didn't belong to her!

Tiffany frowned as she stared down at her hand. For some days she'd been aware of a faint question mark in her mind regarding the slim gold band about her finger. And now, as she gazed down at the ring, set above the knuckle on the fourth finger of her left hand, she tried to concentrate on the problem. Come on! she urged herself roughly. You've got most of your mind back in working order now—so use it!

Ignoring the hustle and bustle of the crowd about her still figure, Tiffany gazed blindly down at her hand and tried to remember every scrap of information she'd been given, particularly about her original discovery by the police at Sintra. She, and everyone else, were agreed that this was *not* her own wedding-ring. In fact, according to the policeman who'd interviewed her in the hospital, Zarco had definitely identified the ring as one belonging to his wife Maxine. But, if that was so—how did it come to be on *her* finger? Looking at the problem from all angles, there could only be one answer: this thin gold band must have been *deliberately* substituted for her own wedding-ring!

For a brief moment it seemed as though the whole world was suddenly turned upside-down. Almost as though she was whirling through space and time as all the disjointed, separate pieces of the jigsaw reformed themselves in her brain.

Although her own had been rather loose, wedding-rings were traditionally difficult to remove from their wearer's fingers. And therefore it must have been Maxine *herself* who had exchanged the rings! Although Tiffany couldn't yet see why—was it something to do with the theft of the gold and jewellery?—she now had no doubts that the other woman had been responsible for the substitution. However, in order to discover the reason which lay behind such a peculiar action, she was going to have to know more about Maxine—and the facts which lay behind her extraordinary-sounding marriage to Zarco.

'*Tiffany*!'

'Mmm . . . ?' She blinked up at the figure standing over her, his broad shoulders silhouetted against the fiery red ball of the setting sun.

'I've been looking for you for the past half-hour,' Zarco told her impatiently, bending down to grasp hold of her arm and drawing her up to her feet. 'It's time for us to go.'

'But I've just realised that——'

'Come along,' he commanded firmly, completely disregarding her muttered protests. 'My son wants to say goodbye to you. Although I can't think why,' he added curtly, striding so fast across the grass that she was almost forced to run to keep up with him.

'Maybe it's because he likes me,' she snapped, her brief spurt of defiance dying away as she saw Charlie standing beside his father's car, his face wreathed in a broad grin. She mustn't upset the boy by quarrelling with his father, she told herself quickly as Zarco's son ran towards her.

'Thanks for helping me with my sums,' he grinned, throwing his thin arms about her waist and giving her a hug. 'I'll write and let you know how I get on.'

She bent down to return the boy's hug. 'I'll look forward to hearing all about it,' she told him with a grin. 'Although I shall take it as a personal insult if you don't get ten out of ten!'

As Zarco steered the vehicle back down the gravelled drive of the school, she turned to wave at the solitary, rather forlorn-looking figure standing outside the school.

'He's such a nice boy. It does seem a pity he has to go to boarding-school,' she murmured. 'Wouldn't he be happier if he could live at home, and go to a nearby day school?'

'When I want your opinion about my son's education, I'll ask for it,' Zarco drawled coldly. 'Until then—why don't you mind your own business?'

Tiffany gasped, feeling as though she'd just had a bucket of cold water thrown over her. 'That's a totally unfair thing to say!' she exclaimed, turning to glare at him.

But Zarco ignored her protest. Clearly immersed in his own deep thoughts, he continued to remain brooding and silent, not uttering another word until he drove the Aston Martin off the main road and down a country lane, before bringing the car to a halt outside a large, ivy-covered restaurant. And even then, after switching off the engine, he continued to stare blindly straight ahead through the windscreen.

It seemed to Tiffany as if the ever increasing sense of menace and claustrophobia within the vehicle was almost tangible. But, just when it seemed to be practically beating on her eardrums, Zarco's hard voice suddenly broke into the oppressive silence.

'What is the square root of one hundred and sixty-nine?'

She frowned and turned to look at him. 'Why on earth do you want to know that?'

'Just answer the question!' he grated harshly.

'It's thirteen, of course.' She shrugged her shoulders. 'Now, do you mind telling me what this is all about?'

He gave a heavy sigh. 'My wife may have been a very clever, tricky woman—but she had one blind spot,' he said in a low, monotonous voice, empty of all expression. 'For some unknown reason, she was completely hopeless at any kind of mathematics.'

'I still don't see ...'

'Maxine had the utmost difficulty with even simple multiplication and division. Anything more complicated would have been totally beyond her,' he replied flatly.

Tiffany gazed at his grim profile, her mind in turmoil. 'So, what you're saying ... you mean that you're now prepared to accept the fact that I'm *not* your wife?' she asked breathlessly.

Zarco continued to stare straight ahead out of the car window, and it was some moments before he broke the tense silence.

'Yes, Tiffany ...' he agreed with a sigh, slowly turning his head to face her. 'I rather think that I do.'

CHAPTER SEVEN

TIFFANY'S brain was still in a chaotic whirl as Zarco got out of the car, and came around to open the passenger door.

That he should have so swiftly capitulated—so quickly changed his mind about her—seemed almost unbelievable. And all because Maxine apparently couldn't add two and two without making five!

'I still don't understand,' she muttered as he bent down to help her from the vehicle. 'Why have you suddenly changed your tune? I've been telling you for weeks that I'm not Maxine, and now—all of a sudden...'

'It isn't all that sudden, of course,' he said, putting a hand on her arm as he led her towards the large building. 'I suppose I must have known the truth for some time. It just happened to be today that I finally realised there was no way you could possibly be Maxine.'

'Well, I suppose I ought to be glad that the penny has dropped at last!' she grumbled, still not really able to believe that her torment was at an end.

'I can understand that you might be justifiably annoyed with me...'

'I certainly am!'

'...and I clearly owe you a very deep and abject apology.'

'You most certainly do!' she snapped, before absorbing the quiet sincerity in his deep voice. Zarco—

actually apologising to her? She turned her head to gaze up at him in astonishment.

'There's no need to look *quite* so surprised!' he told her with a low, rueful laugh. 'I can occasionally admit to being in the wrong.'

It was a struggle, but Tiffany managed to bite back the extremely rude retort which had swiftly risen to her lips. And while she was still staring at him in open-mouthed exasperation he swiftly bent to brush his mouth across her lips.

'I think it might be a good idea to continue any further discussion over a meal, don't you?' he murmured, not giving her time to argue as he led her inside the large building.

It was hopeless. She was never going to understand this man, Tiffany told herself, striving to control the nervous fluttering in her stomach as they entered the restaurant. One moment he was deeply insulting, and then—in the twinkling of an eye—he could give her a kiss, and send her pulses racing out of control.

'But what are we going to do now?' she asked some minutes later, after they'd been shown to a secluded table in the beautifully decorated dining-room of the restaurant.

Zarco didn't reply immediately, and she waited with mounting impatience while he placed their order with the attentive head waiter. He was obviously a well known and valued customer, and there was some considerable discussion about which wines to have with their choice of cold watercress soup and chicken with a tarragon sauce.

She must be careful, Tiffany warned herself grimly. Not only did Zarco use his obvious charm like a weapon—even the waiter appeared to be bowled over by his warm, friendly smile—but it was a charm to which she was also extremely vulnerable. And she knew, only too well, just how this formidable man's dark, sinister attraction could affect her fragile emotions.

'Well . . . ?' Tiffany demanded as the waiter hurried away with their order. 'What am I going to do now? I mean, I haven't really had any time to think about it, but I ought to find myself somewhere to live—possibly in London?' She frowned, brushing a hand through her short, curly hair. 'I'd be grateful if I could borrow some money from you—just to start with, of course—then I ought to look for some kind of job, and——'

'No, I don't think so,' he drawled flatly.

She frowned across the table at him. 'What do you mean?'

'I mean that you aren't going anywhere. Not until we've solved the problem, and recovered my family's jewels, of course.'

'There's no ''of course'' about it!' she flashed back quickly. 'And it's *your* problem, not mine! I didn't ask to be hauled over here, like a badly wrapped parcel, and then treated by you as if I were some sort of criminal,' she added bitterly.

'Nevertheless, here you are and here you stay, until I find out *exactly* what happened in Lisbon,' he told her firmly.

'Oh—*great*!' She glared at him. 'So much for the abject apology!'

He leaned forward, putting his large brown hand over her fingers, which were toying nervously with her cutlery on the table in front of her. 'I think I would prefer to leave that until we return home,' he murmured, giving her a glinting glance from beneath his heavy eyelids which sent shivers quivering up and down her backbone. 'In the meantime, I would suggest that we concentrate on enjoying our meal.'

'Yes, well...' she muttered breathlessly, inching her hand away from beneath his. 'Even if you haven't recovered your beastly jewellery, there are still so many questions which need answering.'

'Such as...?'

'Well—first and foremost is the question of your wife Maxine. I still don't know what happened to me in Lisbon, or why somebody hit me on the head on that cliff-top, but she has to be behind it, doesn't she?'

'Possibly.' He shrugged his shoulders, as if the whole question of his wife bored him rigid.

'There's no possibly about it,' she retorted. 'In fact, I need to know everything you can tell me about that awful woman Maxine dos Santos!'

Zarco's face darkened ominously. However, when Tiffany quickly explained the conclusion she'd come to earlier that afternoon, based on what must have been a *deliberate* exchange of her and Maxine's wedding-rings, he leaned back in his chair, regarding her in a thoughtful silence.

'I know it must be difficult, and maybe even painful for you to have to rehash your past life. But you're the only one who can help to solve this mystery,' she told him quietly. 'Quite apart from anything else, it may also be helpful in locating the stolen gold and jewellery.'

Zarco raised a dark eyebrow. 'I fail to see how a discussion of my private life will aid the return of my lost possessions.'

Relieved to see that he was at least prepared to listen to her, Tiffany decided to place all her cards on the table.

'I've had a lot of time to think about the problem,' she told him with a brief, wry smile. 'In fact, with the loss of part of my memory, I've had very little else to think about! And it seems to me that not only is your wife the central figure in this drama, but it's what you called the "scam"—the theft of your family's valuable jewellery—which lies at the core of the problem. You see,' she added with a shrug, 'I've always had one great advantage over you—I *knew* that I wasn't Maxine. And since *I* wasn't the mastermind behind the burglary, I really do need to know more about the woman who was!'

'And how would that help?' he enquired smoothly.

'Oh, for heaven's sake—surely it's obvious?' she exclaimed. 'There can't be many wives who deliberately set out to steal well over two million pounds' worth of jewellery from their husbands? So, the first question has to be, why should she do such a thing? I mean, even if you don't like each other—which is putting it mildly!—it does seem the most extraordinary thing to do, doesn't it? I don't know how wealthy you are, of course, but surely it would have been easier for her to have had a divorce, and settled for a large amount of alimony?'

Zarco stared silently at her for some moments, before giving a shrug of his broad shoulders.

'You are quite right,' he said at last. 'My wife would be very well off financially, following any divorce settlement.'

'There you are! Not only does the whole scam seem daft—but why should Maxine go to all the trouble of exchanging her wedding-ring for my own?'

He sighed and shook his head, but the arrival of the waiter with their first course prevented him from saying anything further. However, as they consumed the cold watercress soup, he remained buried in thought, until, laying his spoon down on the empty plate, he gave a resigned shrug of his shoulders.

'You are quite right. I do find it painful to think, let alone talk about my past life with my—er—wife,' he told her with a bitter, twisted smile. 'It is a story which reflects very little credit on myself, and absolutely none on Maxine. In fact, like Pandora, I think you will find this is a box that you'll wish you hadn't opened,' he warned grimly.

'I still need to know about her,' Tiffany said stubbornly.

He shrugged. 'What is it you wish to know?'

'I'm not entirely sure.' She gazed at him uncertainly. 'I just feel totally convinced that the answer to your wife's peculiar behaviour has to lie somewhere in the past. And, since we must have met at some time—how else would I have ended up wearing her clothes and her wedding-ring?—maybe something you say will help the missing part of my memory to return.'

'Very well—on your own head be it!' Zarco's jaw clenched and his lips tightened for a moment, as if bracing himself for an ordeal. 'I can give you very few details about Maxine's early life,' he began slowly, before relating part of the information which she'd been given by the psychoanalyst in the hospital in Lisbon.

'However,' he continued, 'Maxine's father—a most highly respected and respectable bank manager—has since told me that she was always very wild when young. Apparently, she ran away from boarding-school at the age of seventeen, her father and stepmother losing all track of her for some years—despite all their efforts to discover her whereabouts. It was only when her stepmother opened a magazine that they eventually discovered that she was a fashion model in New York.'

It really was the most extraordinary sensation, Tiffany decided, to listen to the story of a woman who was not only her double, but about whom she knew so little.

Maxine, it seemed, had by then already married her first husband—an American of Italian descent called Antonio Salvatore. Because it was shortly after contacting his daughter in New York that Maxine's father learned that she had become a widow.

'That is a period of my wife's life about which I know very little, and which my agents are investigating at this moment,' Zarco told her, not bothering to hide his clear conviction that Maxine's hitherto unknown life in New York would also turn out to be yet another discreditable can of worms.

'Surely Maxine must have done *something* decent in her life?'

'If she has, I have yet to hear about it!' he retorted curtly, before explaining that his wife had left America on the death of her first husband, flying down to Brazil to stay with her father in São Paulo, the business centre of that huge country.

Unfortunately, it seemed that the return of the prodigal daughter had not been a success. Certainly not as far as her father and stepmother were concerned. From what Tiffany could gather, there appeared to have been several unsavoury incidents, about which Zarco refused to give her any details, merely relating the fact that Maxine had led a thoroughly wild, dissipated life, which had horrified her respectable and somewhat strait-laced parents. However, he had known nothing of Maxine's debauched lifestyle. He'd only been aware that a business friend of his possessed a daughter—an attractive widow to whom he'd been briefly introduced at a large cocktail party.

'It was some years since my first wife, Charlotte, had died. And yet, pathetic as it may seem to you, I was still very much in love with her memory,' Zarco remarked flatly, before lapsing into a long and withdrawn silence.

'I don't think it sounds pathetic,' Tiffany assured him softly, her heart wrung by the deep note of past misery and unhappiness in his voice. 'I think that what you have just said must be just about the greatest compliment a man could pay his wife.'

'You think so?' he murmured, and for the first time that she could remember Zarco's hard and formidable guard seemed to be momentarily lowered. His dark handsome features softened, and for a few brief seconds Tiffany glimpsed quite another and much softer personality.

But then his iron control reasserted itself as he slowly and with obvious discomfiture began to relate the events leading up to his marriage to Maxine— events which he clearly felt to be shameful and humiliating.

He was still mourning his dead wife, and, apart from burying himself in work, Zarco had been content to spend all his free time with his small son, who was cared for by a houseful of servants at his large home in São Paulo. However, his many friends were convinced that he was working too hard, and had persuaded him to take a brief holiday in Rio de Janeiro, during the Carnival.

The holiday had not been a success. Mostly because, as he explained, he had still felt very much alone, despite the frantic noise and spectacle of the celebrations. So it was perhaps inevitable that on his last night in Rio Zarco had taken refuge in the bar of his luxury hotel, drowning his sorrows in alcohol. When he had awoken the next morning, it was to find a girl sleeping beside him—a girl of whom he had absolutely no recollection whatsoever.

'I had dearly loved Charlotte, and felt sincere grief over her loss, but...' A faint flush tinged Zarco's high cheekbones as he confessed to not remaining celibate in the years following his first wife's death. 'I'm a mere mortal man—and certainly no monk!' he informed Tiffany, a wry smile touching his lips as he viewed her blush of embarrassment.

Emphasising that his brief affairs had been conducted with older, sophisticated women who were no more serious than he was, Zarco admitted that he'd been distressed and deeply ashamed to discover the girl beside him in the hotel bedroom. He truly didn't recollect ever having seen her before, and, suffering from a monumental hangover, he'd apologised to the girl for anything that might have happened, and sent her on her way.

It wasn't until some weeks after his return to São Paulo that the girl—who was, of course, Maxine—had contacted him. Revealing her identity, and claiming that she was pregnant with his child, she had demanded that he 'do the right thing' and marry her.

Zarco had realised that he'd no choice in the matter. Not only was Maxine the daughter of a *very* respectable English bank manager, but Zarco was also burdened by a deep sense of guilt at having ruined a girl's life by his careless, drunken behaviour. Moreover, as he firmly pointed out to Tiffany, his own personal code of honour as a gentleman had left him no option: he must marry the young widow who was expecting his child.

'We had just begun our honeymoon when my new wife informed me that, just prior to our hastily arranged marriage, she'd arranged to have her pregnancy terminated.'

'But . . . but that's *terrible*! How could she do such a dreadful thing?' Tiffany gasped, her soft heart aching at the obvious pain behind Zarco's harsh words and his bleak, stony expression.

'It has since occurred to me, of course, that she might not have been pregnant at all. I did subsequently discover that she'd been on the look-out for a rich husband, a fact underlined a year or two ago when, in one of her violent rages, Maxine confessed that she had deliberately followed me to Rio—with the express intention of ending up in my bed.'

'Oh, Zarco—how awful! You must have been *so* unhappy,' Tiffany breathed, appalled and horrified by the story of his forced marriage.

'Yes, it is not a pretty story,' he sighed deeply. 'The intolerable situation was not helped, of course, by the realisation that I only had myself to blame. And when I found myself locked into the prison of my marriage, I buried myself in work and spent as much time abroad as I could. My sole concern, of course, has always been the welfare of my son. So, when I inherited Norton Manor a few years ago, I subsequently placed Carlos in his boarding-school, and have virtually seen nothing of my wife—not until I received the news of her accident, in Lisbon.'

'You must have known that wasn't me!' she cried huskily, oblivious of the other people in the dining-room. 'I could never——'

'Hush! You must not raise your voice in here, like this,' he cautioned, clasping hold of her hand once more, and holding it firmly while signalling to a passing waiter.

'But I've never heard such a terrible story!' she exclaimed helplessly in a low voice, her cheeks flushing with embarrassment as she belatedly realised they were being regarded with some interest by the people dining at a nearby table. 'I could *never* have behaved in such a disgusting, foul way towards anyone—let alone trap them into such a dreadful travesty of a marriage!'

'Well, perhaps this is the right time to say that——' He was interrupted by the arrival of the waiter, who placed a large glass of brandy down on the table in front of her. 'Drink it up!' he commanded as she gazed dubiously down at the amber liquid in the balloon-shaped glass.

'I really don't think——'

'Do as I say!' he grated, frowning with concern as he viewed the girl's pale cheeks, and her visibly trembling figure.

The Aston Martin purred its way through the small country villages, its pearl-grey exterior shimmering ghostily in the light of the full moon. Having left the restaurant, Zarco had obviously decided to take a more winding route back to Norton Manor.

Tiffany turned to steal a quick, fleeting glance through her eyelashes at Zarco's stern profile, illuminated by the light from the streetlamps of a small village. He had been strangely silent and withdrawn since they had left the restaurant. Not unfriendly, but somehow distant and obviously preoccupied with his own thoughts. It was as though he had much to think about—as, indeed, had she.

As Tiffany leaned back on the comfortable leather seat of the fast car, speeding along the country roads, she had to admit that Zarco had been quite right. The consumption of such a large amount of brandy—especially since she wasn't used to strong drink—had definitely made her feel a good deal better. And, although nothing could diminish her basic revulsion at learning of Maxine's behaviour, she also had to admit that Zarco had done his best to soothe her lacerated feelings.

As he had pointed out, his marriage had taken place several years ago. 'I have had a long time to think things over, and to realise that my life wasn't a total tragedy—not when I had my much loved son to care for. I simply made the mistake of picking a rotten apple from the barrel of life. It could have happened to anyone,' he'd added with a rueful shrug of his broad shoulders, before deliberately changing the subject.

Refusing to discuss any further the vexed question of his wife, Zarco had proved to be an attentive and amusing companion during the remainder of their meal in the restaurant. Not drinking himself, because he was driving, he'd nevertheless made sure that her own wine glass was replenished. Which had not been a very good idea, if the fumes of alcohol now swirling around her brain were anything to go by! But, whether or not it was the effect of the wine and brandy which she'd consumed, there was no doubt that she had swiftly fallen a willing victim to the beguiling force of his overwhelming attraction.

In fact, you allowed him to charm the socks off you! Tiffany was telling herself with disgust as the car swept down over the gravelled drive towards the front door of Norton Manor. But even knowing how feebly she'd caved in to his dark enchantment couldn't seem to dent her extraordinary sense of happiness and euphoria as he led her inside the old house.

Luckily, Amy Long had left a tray containing a Thermos of hot coffee in the drawing-room. And while Zarco left her for a few minutes, to check on some business matter in the library, Tiffany hurriedly poured herself a cup of liquid caffeine.

Unfortunately, even with the assistance of black coffee, her mind simply didn't seem to be responding to the alarm bells which were ringing at the back of her head. And telling herself that she was crazy—that she was on a one-way ticket to disaster and deep unhappiness—couldn't seem to puncture her crazy mood of elation and intoxication.

Intoxication was absolutely the right word! She *must* sober up! Tiffany warned herself grimly. Because, if she didn't watch out, it looked as if she was in grave danger of losing her head—and her heart—to the man who had so dominated her life over the last month.

She ought to hate Zarco, especially when she remembered just how abominably he had behaved towards her. But no wise words or stern warnings seemed to have any effect on the deep tide of sick excitement which seemed to be flowing through her veins. Even thinking about his broad shoulders and his long, lean legs was enough to bring on a case of the hot flushes! In fact, if strong liquor and a brief exposure to Zarco's hypnotic charm could produce this sort of effect on her, she was undoubtedly in *deep* trouble, she thought wildly.

'Ah, is that for me?' Zarco said, coming into the room and sitting down beside her. 'I've just been checking my fax machine,' he told her, his eyes glinting with amusement as he took the cup and saucer from her nervous, trembling hands.

A silence fell in the room as she stared down at her lap, trying to avoid looking at the man who was sitting so close to her. All the physical sensations she had come to associate with Zarco, whenever she was in close proximity to his tall figure, had returned with a vengeance: her pulse was racing out of control, her mouth was dry, and her skin was burning although she felt as cold as ice.

'And did baring my soul tonight, at dinner, give you any answers to the questions in your mind?' he enquired smoothly.

'No, I'm afraid it didn't,' she muttered huskily. 'But—er—I really ought to thank you for the lovely meal, although I'm afraid that I must have drunk far too much wine,' she added, turning to glance at him.

'Really?' he drawled mockingly, his voice heavy with amusement as he leaned back in the sofa and smiled at her.

With one of the inexplicable, violent mood swings which had been affecting her lately, Tiffany found herself glaring at his handsome, tanned face. It was just one of his usual megawatt smiles, she told herself furiously. It was hardly the end of the world! And why its mesmerising effect should be causing her to feel totally spaced-out she had absolutely no idea.

'I—er—I think it's time I went to bed,' she mumbled nervously, desperately trying to tear her gaze away from the disturbing gleam in his dark eyes, their brilliant glitter carrying a message that was making her head swim. She could feel a deep throbbing excitement in the pit of her stomach, and a disturbing mixture of emotions that swung wildly between fear and awareness, sending prickles of apprehension tingling down the length of her spine.

'What a good idea! I think I'll join you,' he drawled blandly, although he made no effort to rise from the sofa.

A sudden surge of panic caused her to snap, 'Not in my bed, you won't!' before a deep tide of crimson swamped her pale cheeks. 'What I meant was, I . . . I don't want to put up with any more of your nonsense!'

He gave a dry snort of laughter. 'My nonsense?'

'You know *exactly* what I mean,' she protested, making a valiant effort to close her mind to the memory of her helpless response to his cynical love-making only a few days ago. 'To put it bluntly, I don't want you anywhere near my bedroom.'

'Are you sure?' he murmured slowly, his mouth curving into a wide, sensual grin.

'Absolutely certain!' she lied firmly, clinging on to her feelings of anger about the way this man had used her as if to a lifebelt.

She should have heeded the warning gleam in his eyes. But Tiffany was far too pleased with herself for having, at last, been firm with the obnoxious man, and was caught unawares as Zarco's hand snaked out to grab hold of her wrist—and a moment later she found herself suddenly pulled into his arms.

Dazed to find her slender body trapped within his firm embrace, she couldn't prevent herself from trembling violently, her pulses throbbing wildly out of control. She stared into his eyes, her heightened senses overwhelmingly aware of the warm musky scent of his male body, the faint flush on his high cheek-bones beneath the smooth tanned skin, and the dark curly hair at the base of the strong brown column of his throat rising from his open-necked shirt.

And then his dark head came down towards her. 'You're such a little liar, Tiffany...!' The words whispered against her soft lips were tantalising, causing her to quiver and shake with a deep and urgent need as his lips gently traced the shape of her mouth. His ragged breath and the fast, irregular thudding of his heart was echoed by her own body, and she was shaken to the core as she realised he was right. It was far too late to warn herself against losing her head and her heart to this man. She was already fathoms deep in love with him.

With her last ounce of control, she tried to push him away, her panic and protest lost beneath his mouth as he stormed her defences, his deepening kiss sending waves of fire pulsating through her body. And then slowly, very slowly, the relentless pressure of his lips eased, and he raised his head to stare down at her in silence, lifting a hand to gently brush the soft wavy curls from her brow. There was a deep hunger in the eyes devouring her pale face, and in the fingers which shook slightly as they brushed across her soft skin.

'Please, Zarco—let me go!' she pleaded, her voice husky with desire. But when she saw the sensual mockery in his brief smile, and the glittering darkness of his eyes beneath their heavy lids, she knew there was about as much chance of her wish being granted as there was of an eagle releasing its prey. His next words confirmed it.

'You aren't going anywhere—except to my bed!' he growled, the hoarse determination in his voice causing sensual images to flood her mind. Pulsating waves of heat seemed to scorch through every part of her body as, with effortless ease, he rose from the sofa and carried her limp, trembling form out of the room, across the hall and up the wide curving staircase to his bedroom.

Never having dared approach this wing of the old house, which was always firmly guarded by a heavy carved oak door, Tiffany had a confused impression of the large room as she found herself being lowered down on to a wide bed. The soft light of the lamps glowed warmly against the strong colours of deep red and blue with which his bedroom was decorated. And then her bemused vision was filled by his dark handsome face as he leaned over her.

'*Deus*—I want you!' he groaned deep in his throat, swiftly undoing his shirt and throwing it aside before turning his attention to her blouse. Cursing under his breath at having to deal with the tiny pearl buttons, he impetuously ripped the garment apart, his action causing her to tremble and shiver at the force which lay behind his raging impatience.

'I can't . . .' she moaned, a muscle beating convulsively in her throat. 'Brian always said I was hopeless . . . and I don't really know how to——'

'Hush, beloved,' Zarco murmured gently, gazing down into the girl's bemused sapphire-blue eyes, and the hectic flush now covering her cheeks. 'Your husband . . . ? He was not kind to you, in bed?'

She shook her head. 'No . . .' she whispered miserably. 'But it was all my fault, you see. I couldn't relax . . . and then he always became so cross . . . so angry, and . . .'

She clamped her eyes shut with embarrassment, almost flinching as she waited for Zarco to reject her, as Brian had done in the past. But then she felt his warm arms tenderly enfolding her trembling body, drawing her gently into his embrace.

'You have no need to worry, my sweet one,' he murmured, his voice husky with desire. 'Your late husband was obviously a foolish man—and it is now my good fortune to teach you the delights of the flesh, yes?' he breathed, before beginning to kiss her very softly, his lips seeming to carry a magic spell as they trailed slowly down over her face and throat to her breasts.

The feel of his warm mouth and hands on her bare flesh sent quivers of excitement dancing across her skin once more. Beneath the mastery of his touch she gradually lost all fear. She was swept by a need to feel his bare body against her, the tactile warmth of his skin pressed close to her own; to savour the mind-bending sensations of his hands and mouth on her flesh.

Gradually, the rising sexual tension began flooding through her stomach, swelling the soft curves of her full breasts, and causing her to move wantonly beneath him, in a silent plea to be freed of the remaining barriers between them.

Her emotions were spinning out of control—and she simply didn't care! She seemed to be held fast within the grip of a languid, yielding and timeless force which drove out all fear of the past and the future. The only hard reality was here and now; the urge to lift her trembling hands to the dark curly hair of his broad chest, to slide her fingertips over the tiny, damp beads of moisture on his skin, and to feel the warmth of the firm flesh over his hard, muscular torso. She revelled in his strength as her fingers explored the smooth length of his back, the sound of his husky groan at her touch as he swiftly removed the last barrier of her thin silk underwear, inciting her to press her quivering lips against the smooth column of his throat, her mouth savouring the peppery male taste and scent of his skin.

'*Deus . . . Deus*!' he breathed as he swiftly removed the rest of his own clothing. 'I've wanted you for so long,' he whispered, the deep, huskily sensual note in his voice inflaming her desire.

She was totally seduced by his mouth, moving without haste slowly down over her body, exploring each soft curve and crevice, the heat of his tongue flicking erotically over her tautly swollen nipples, exploring her navel with a teasing sensuality. Every nerve in her body seemed to be throbbing in response to the arousing, voluptuous touch of his lips as he kissed each one of her pink toes, leisurely brushing his mouth over her insteps and up over the soft, velvety skin behind her knees and on towards her trembling thighs.

She felt as though she was drowning—drowning in ecstasy as his hands, lips and tongue continued to caress and arouse her body. Love for him seemed to produce an overwhelming, surging passion in which there could be no resistance, no holding back. She wanted to express her joy, to cry out that she loved him beyond anything in the world, but her dazed mind seemed incapable of finding the words to express her feelings. And then there was no time for conscious thought as she writhed and moaned helplessly beneath his intimate touch.

His fingers and mouth were stroking her, leading her upwards towards some hitherto unknown pinnacle of bliss and passion, a faint film of perspiration covering her skin as she heard a voice she hardly recognised as her own calling out helplessly as the rhythm increased to become a frenzy inside her, before she was suddenly seized by an endless series of mounting convulsions, soaring up into such a transport of ecstasy and delight that she was certain that she would faint or die at any moment.

It was only then that his tall figure swiftly covered hers with a dynamic urgency, and she welcomed his hard, powerful thrust and the devastating, forceful rhythm of his vigorous body, lifting them both upwards to the stratosphere. The muscles in his arms and throat were projecting tautly, straining like cords of steel until at last he, too, groaned in the release and ecstasy of their mutual fulfilment.

Later, as she lay happily wrapped in his embrace, vibrantly aware that Zarco's lovemaking far transcended anything she could ever have imagined, Tiffany gave a small sigh of deep and total contentment, before slowly drifting into a dreamless sleep.

Hours later, when she awoke to find herself still cradled in his arms, it was to see the grey fingers of dawn stealing in through the window. She lay for a time quietly listening to the strong, rhythmic beat of his heart.

She hadn't realised that Zarco was also awake, not until he whispered in her ear, 'Are you content, little one?'

'Mmm...' she murmured, still in that blissful, delicious state of not being quite awake.

'I wanted you,' he whispered, his hands beginning to move slowly and sensually over her body. 'From the first moment I saw you in the hospital, I knew I *must* have you!' he added, pressing his lips to the soft flesh of her shoulders.

It was the word 'hospital' which broke through to register in her sleepy mind. And even as she responded to the touch of his fingers, which were now softly stroking the sensitive tips of her breasts, she was suddenly swamped by a cold tidal wave of harsh reality.

'Oh, no—we can't...we mustn't do this!' she gasped, beginning to struggle in his arms. 'I'm not your wife, and——'

'I thank God that you are not!' he whispered against her skin, his fingers continuing to caress her body, which quivered at his sensual touch.

'But don't you see? We can't do this—it's quite wrong!' she cried, fear and misery lending her a strength she didn't know she possessed as she pushed him away from her. 'Maxine is still your wife! And so this...this is *adultery*!'

'Maxine has *never* been a true wife to me!' he growled bitterly. 'And, since you tell me that your husband is dead, how can our lovemaking be called adultery?' he demanded, sitting up and pushing a forceful, angry hand through his roughly tousled dark hair.

But Tiffany knew she mustn't listen to him; that she was far too vulnerable to the siren-song of his dark attraction. With an enormous effort, she forced herself to concentrate all her energies on scrambling quickly from the bed, because if she didn't do so immediately she knew it would be too late.

'No. No, we can't...we mustn't do this! It's quite, quite wrong,' she sobbed, running blindly towards the door, tears streaming down her face at the realisation that, however much she loved this man, they could never, ever have any future together.

CHAPTER EIGHT

THE early morning sun was beginning to rise up over the horizon.

Walking slowly over the wide green lawn, Tiffany's bare feet left clearly discernible footprints on the grass, which was still heavy with dew. But not as heavy as her heart, she told herself with a deep shuddering sigh, her tired and weary eyes barely able to absorb the tranquil scene of woodland and meadows stretching out before her.

It had, without a doubt, been, at one and the same time, quite the most wonderful and yet the very worst night of her life. She ought to be glad that Zarco had made no move to prevent her from leaving, or to follow her sobbing figure as she had fled from his bedroom. But, perversely, she'd desperately hoped that he would. His presence would at least have been proof that she meant something more to him than just a brief, fleeting desire for her body. But she couldn't fool herself. He had never, at any time, either said or intimated that he loved her.

For one brief moment, when she'd turned in the open doorway before leaving his room, she had seen his face illuminated by a grey shaft of early morning light stealing in through the open, mullioned windows of his room. His chiselled features, highlighted by the pale light of day, had looked drawn and haggard, and she could almost have deceived herself into believing that it was pain she'd seen in his eyes. But, of course, she quickly told herself, she must have been mistaken.

A sharp, agonising spasm gripped her stomach for a moment. It seemed impossible that she could ever be able to forget the total joy and ecstasy which she had experienced in Zarco's strong arms last night. And yet, having discovered the rapture and delight of his lovemaking, she now found herself burdened by a deep, heavy sense of wrongdoing. She didn't even have the excuse of not knowing that he was a married man. Who better than *she* to know the truth about his desperately unhappy state of wedlock?

And always in the forefront of her mind, and in every fibre of her trembling body, was the realisation—when it was now far too late—that she had fallen deeply and hopelessly in love, with a man who could never reciprocate her feelings—or make her his lawful wife.

Despite her lack of sleep, and the throbbing, pounding headache which was causing her to wince at the glare of the bright, early morning sun, Tiffany's brain was still capable of functioning normally. Totally sick at heart, she was torn between her common sense and her turbulent emotions. Although it was the last thing in the world that she wanted, she knew that she had no choice: she must leave Norton Manor as soon as she could—today, if possible. Because, if she'd wanted to run away before, to escape from the imprisonment forced on her by Zarco's mistaken identification, she was doubly determined to do so now.

There was nothing to keep her here. No excuse for Zarco to continue to maintain that she was his wife— a fact which she had always known to be false. And, now that he was firmly convinced that she was not

Maxine, Tiffany knew that she no longer had any reason to remain in this lovely old medieval manor house.

At the thought of Maxine, her mouth tightened. She felt a deep, simmering fury at having been so contemptuously used as a mere pawn by the other woman. And, although she still didn't know how or why, she was quite convinced that Zarco's wife had been the main force behind what was clearly a very complicated, well planned and well executed theft. If she should ever meet Maxine, she'd cheerfully plunge a knife into the other woman's black heart, Tiffany told herself with grim relish.

However, indulging in the fantasy of an extremely painful and clearly well deserved fate for the other woman wasn't going to achieve anything. In fact, even if the dreadful woman had never existed, and the meeting between her and Zarco had occurred in another time and place, he would still have been way out of her reach. Their relationship could never have had a happy ending—even if he'd been free and unencumbered by a wife. Because, if she was to be sensible and honest with herself, Zarco was totally out of her class.

What did she, who came from a very ordinary background and who'd been married to an unsuccessful tennis player, have in common with an extremely wealthy Brazilian aristocrat? Although they had both been swept by a sudden mutual passion for each other, it couldn't last. The white heat of overwhelming desire would soon have faded, and when it did—as it must inevitably—what would they have left between them? Tiffany knew nothing of his social world, or his business life, and would have found herself like a fish out of water. His smart friends would have looked at her askance, and she'd have been unhappy and uncomfortable in his obviously glamorous, sophisticated world.

So maybe his realisation that she was not his wife had come just in time to save them both from a dreadful mistake?

But, as Tiffany grimly acknowledged, it was one thing to give herself a stern, moral and sensible lecture—and quite another to try and force her wounded heart to accept the level-headed, practical good sense behind her reasoning. Instinctively she knew that Zarco was her first and only love. She would never be able to feel for anyone else the deep, overwhelming intensity of emotion that she felt for him; even when she was old and grey the thought of his tall, dark and handsome figure would always cause her heart to miss a beat.

As she was almost drowning in misery and despondency, it was some time before Tiffany registered the brief, jerky movements on the periphery of her vision. Frowning, she paused and peered through the early morning mist towards the dovecot. Surely... surely that had been the figure of a man which she'd just seen disappearing behind the ancient circular brick and stone structure?

However, as she moved slowly towards the dovecot, past the neatly clipped yew hedge, she realised that she must have been mistaken. There was no sign of anyone or anything—other than a frightened rabbit, which scampered quickly out of her way as she walked around the outside of the building.

She was just telling herself that it must have been a figment of her overheated imagination when a hand suddenly flashed through the half-open door of the dovecot, roughly grabbing her arm and dragging her inside.

Taken unawares, Tiffany gave a muffled shriek as she was spun around, and practically thrown against the rough brickwork inside the old structure. She was gasping with fright, and it was some time before her eyes became used to the murky darkness, barely pierced by the pale glimmer of daylight coming from the many small, round holes high up in the wall. She could only see the outline of a man silhouetted against the light from the open doorway, her legs trembling as her mind registered the threatening stance of the figure now moving slowly towards her.

'So, you thought you could dump me—huh?' the man growled. 'Well, I ain't being double-crossed—not by you, or by anyone else!'

Tiffany could feel her legs trembling. There was something about that voice that seemed familiar... The sound of the harsh, nasal twang was causing her to shiver and shake as if she had a fever.

'Yeah! It's me, honey!' The man gave an evil laugh as he came to a halt in front of her nervous, shaking figure. 'But I'm here to tell ya, Maxine, baby, that you don't get rid of your old man that easily!' He gave a snigger. 'Here I am—and here I stay, until I get what I've come for!'

As the man took another step forward, his squat, ugly figure was illuminated by pale shafts of light from the small openings, high above his head.

'T-Tony...!' she gasped as a blinding flash seemed to zigzag through her brain like forked lightning. Once again she could see in her mind's eye the back of his curly head topped by a grey peaked cap as he sat in the front of a large limousine. 'I saw you...in Lisbon!'

'Yeah, yeah!' he muttered impatiently. 'I guess the fact that I'm here is one nasty surprise as far as you're concerned, right? Well, that's just your tough luck, Maxine, baby!'

'You're making a terrible mistake!' Tiffany protested breathlessly. 'I'm not Maxine. She's completely disappeared, and...' She faltered as he threw back his head and gave a peal of raucous laughter.

'Tell that to the Marines, honey!' he said, before the smile was wiped off his face as he took a menacing step towards her. 'I reckon it's time to stop fooling around, huh? I want my share of the loot— and I want it right now!'

'I don't know what you're talking about.' She flinched, cowering against the wall as he grimaced, and jabbed an angry finger towards her. 'I don't have any loot, and...and I promise you—I'm truly *not* Maxine!' she cried helplessly, her eyes skidding nervously about the empty building, looking in vain for some avenue of escape.

'Hey—you're really into this crazy act of yours, aren't you?' Tony shrugged. 'So—OK, I'm a reasonable sorta guy. All I'm saying is, a wife should share things with her husband, right? So, I'll guarantee to keep out of the way, and not to spoil your little game—but I ain't going anywhere, not without what's owing to me.'

'I don't understand...' Tiffany whimpered. 'You're not married to Maxine!'

'Oh, no?' Tony grinned wickedly at her. 'Well, I'd say that having two husbands is *definitely* one too many, honey! But I guess that's your problem—right?

So let's cut out all this nonsense. Just give me my share of the loot, and then I'll disappear like a good little boy.'

Tiffany had given up trying to understand what he was talking about. All she was concerned about was the burning question of how she could escape from this frightening, evil man. But as soon as she took even a small, sideways step, she saw that he was watching her like a hawk. Whoever Tony might be, he clearly had no intention of letting her go. But how was she to get out of here? He seemed totally obsessed by what he called 'the loot'. So, maybe...?

'I—er—I don't have the loot hidden in here,' she began tentatively.

He grinned. 'That's better. I thought I could get you to see sense. So, where is it?'

Tiffany stared at him blankly for a moment. How big was 'the loot' supposed to be? 'Er—it's in the house,' she muttered, 'and I'll have to go there to get your—er—share.'

'OK, I'll buy that,' Tony nodded slowly. 'Got the jewellery hidden away in a safe place, have you?'

Jewellery? Did that mean that Tony was also involved in the theft from Zarco's safety deposit box? But what had he got to do with Maxine?

'Well...?' Tony demanded impatiently.

'Oh—er—yes, it's in the house,' Tiffany agreed quickly.

'And the gold too?'

She nodded fervently. 'Yes—it's all there.'

'So—what are we waiting for? Let's you and me go and get it, honey!' he laughed, quickly reaching forward to grab hold of her arm and dragging her reluctant figure out of the dovecot, across the wide green lawns towards the house.

If *only* she could somehow attract Zarco's attention! Tiffany told herself desperately as she hung back, trying to delay their progress as long as possible. But it was no good. He would still be asleep in his bedroom, on the far side of the house, she realised with a sinking heart.

And then—quite miraculously!—as they neared the old building, she saw the front door being thrown open to disclose Zarco, a furious scowl on his face as he stood framed in the doorway, clothed only in a short towelling dressing-gown.

'Help! *Help me!*' she cried, wrenching her arm away from Tony's grip before taking to her heels and racing towards the security of that tall, dominant figure who had, surprisingly, made no movement towards her. 'It's Tony! He wants the jewellery that Maxine stole from you!' she yelled.

So intent on escaping from Tony, and reaching the safe haven of Zarco's arms, she had no thought or eyes for anyone else. As her bare feet sped across the soft, cushiony surface of the wet grass, she couldn't stop her rapid motion when she reached the gravelled drive.

She barely heard Zarco's shout of warning, nor the sound of the post office van, roaring up the drive to deliver that morning's letters.

The toot of the horn came too late for Tiffany to save herself. As her wet feet slid out from beneath her, she was struck a light, glancing blow by the wing of the vehicle, which tossed her backwards like a rag doll. A brief second later, her head hit the hard surface of the drive with a heavy thump, and as the world seemed to spin dizzily on its axis she was sucked down into a dark, swirling void.

She woke once, her confused mind having an impression of being inside a moving vehicle, and of bright lights slanting down into her dazed eyes, before she lapsed back into unconsciousness again.

When she awoke for a second time, Tiffany immediately knew where she was. It might not be Portugal—and from the sound of a high-pitched English voice next door it certainly wasn't—but hospitals seemed to be the same the world over.

And maybe it was the association with the hospital, in Lisbon, but she realised that she could now easily remember everything which had happened to her in the city—the meeting with Maxine; the destruction of her room in the hotel; her trip to the Quinta dos Santos in Sintra . . . even that desperate struggle on the edge of the cliff, when she'd been so nearly killed by Zarco's wife and Tony.

But *why*? The question seemed to be burning in her brain as she struggled to fit all the pieces of the complicated jigsaw together. But it was hopeless. She couldn't even remember why she was now lying here, in a hospital.

Raising a trembling hand to her head, she sighed with relief to find that she *wasn't* wearing a bandage. In fact, as her trembling fingers explored her head, she discovered that apart from a large, sore lump on her forehead, a splitting headache and a painful shoulder, she seemed to be all right.

The entry of a young, white-coated doctor, and his reassuring words, put her mind to rest.

'It seems you were in a collision with a post van,' he told her with a grin. 'And, although you've only had a mild concussion, your past history of a blow to your head, followed by temporary amnesia, means that we think you ought to have some tests. Just to make sure you're as fit as you look!' he added reassuringly, before his bleeper urgently called him to the aid of another patient.

The departure of the doctor seemed to set in train a series of flying trips around the various departments of the hospital. Checking her from tip to toe, all the various experts pronounced themselves satisfied, but she was left feeling desperately tired and exhausted.

'I'm going to give you a mild injection—just to help you to sleep,' the doctor told her as she was wheeled back into her room. 'You'll feel much better tomorrow morning.'

He was quite right, she realised, surfacing the next day as a pretty young nurse bustled into the room.

'And how are we feeling today, Mrs dos Santos?'

'All right, although my head and shoulder are still very sore,' Tiffany muttered, deciding that she really didn't feel strong enough to resume all the old arguments about the fact that she wasn't Maxine.

'I'm not surprised. You had a very nasty accident,' the nurse told her, coming over to take her pulse and temperature. 'Doctor says that you're going to have to stay here for another day, just until he's checked all the results of your tests.'

'I—er—I forgot to ask—exactly where am I?'

'This is the private wing of St Thomas's Hospital,' the nurse told her. 'And when you get out of bed you'll have a really wonderful view across the River Thames to the Houses of Parliament,' the girl added, going over to pull the curtains well clear of the large window.

'I wish I knew what I was doing here.' Tiffany frowned, unable to remember anything other than Tony's threatening behaviour in the dovecot, and her mad dash across the lawns of Norton Manor towards the safety of Zarco's tall figure.

'Your husband had you transferred up here by private ambulance from the casualty department of your local hospital. I'm sure he'll be pleased to hear that you're doing so well.'

Will he? Tiffany wondered, her fingers nervously winding themselves in the thin hospital blanket. 'I know I've been unconscious for a while, but I don't remember seeing him here, in the hospital . . . ?' she murmured tentatively.

'Oh, well—I expect he's been busy at work. You know what men are like!' The nurse smiled at her comfortingly.

But the other girl's words had confirmed Tiffany's worst suspicions. Zarco *hadn't* been to see her. Was he already regretting their passionate lovemaking? Maybe this was the perfect opportunity for him to get rid of her, she thought miserably, the painful ache beginning to pound in her head once more.

When the doctor came to see her that evening, confirming that she'd been given a clean bill of health by the neurology department, she told him that she wanted to discharge herself.

'Oh, we can't have you doing that,' he told her firmly. 'I understand that arrangements have already been made to take you home tomorrow. So, just be a good girl, and take things easy for the next few days,' he murmured, before whisking himself out of the room to see to his other patients.

What home? she thought dismally. Norton Manor certainly wasn't her home. And, since Zarco hadn't bothered to visit her here in the hospital, it was obvious that he didn't want to have anything more to do with her.

Of all the trials and tribulations which she had suffered over the past month or so, Zarco's abandonment and desertion of her now—at a time when she desperately needed the warmth and comfort of his presence—seemed the unkindest cut of all. Surely he could have spared her just a few moments of his precious time? Even if only to say goodbye...?

The sleeping pill which Tiffany been given that night completely failed to send her to sleep.

Maybe it was her over-active brain which was to blame for her restless state, as she tossed and turned through the endless hours before dawn. Trying to think how she could escape from being taken back to Norton Manor, and having to suffer an emotionally fraught, humiliating farewell scene with Zarco, Tiffany kept coming up against the same obstacles: she had no money, no clothes and no personal identification. And, without any of those three important items, she was well and truly stuck!

The clothes question was temporarily solved the next morning, when a suitcase was delivered to her room containing a sapphire-blue summer dress and matching jacket. However, while resigned to her unhappy fate, Tiffany's spirits took a further dive when she looked at herself in the mirror. The sleepless night was reflected in her pale, chalky white cheeks and the dark shadows beneath her tired blue eyes. She looked *awful*! But there was nothing she could do about it, since whoever had packed her case—probably Amy Long, now she came to think about it—had totally failed to include any make-up.

Not that it mattered all that much, of course, but if she was going to have to face an embarrassing scene with Zarco she would have been grateful for at least the help of some lipstick. The sight of her looking like this was only going to confirm the wisdom of Zarco's obvious decision to get rid of her as quickly as possible.

With a heavy heart, Tiffany accompanied the nurse down in the lift, and out through the main entrance to the hospital.

Last night, she'd thought of a wild scheme of trying to gain the nurse's help; of begging the other girl to lend her some money, so that she could slip away to a small hotel before getting a job, in London. But the cold light of day had shown her the futility of such an idea. Even her belated attempt to ask the doctor to phone Zarco, and tell him not to bother to have her picked up, had been greeted with a laugh—as though she'd been attempting to be funny. Which was a joke in itself, she thought gloomily. Humour was just about the last thing one needed in any dealings with that hard, dangerous man, Zarco dos Santos!

And she might have known her pathetic attempts to escape their last meeting would be doomed to failure. Because as the nurse led her across to a large black limousine she saw Tom Long in his chauffeur's uniform holding the rear door open for her.

Sitting in solitary magnificence in the back of the large vehicle, she was grateful to Tom for not engaging her in conversation during the lonely journey back to Norton Manor. She was feeling too distraught for social niceties, and by the time they rolled up the drive she was in a dire state of nervous tension.

At the sound of the vehicle, Amy came hurrying out on to the steps, anxious to welcome her home.

'The master is still away in Amsterdam, on business. However, I've faithfully promised that I'll look after you until his return,' she assured Tiffany, clucking her teeth with distress at the obvious strain on the girl's pale face.

'It's up to bed with you—and no arguments!' the housekeeper said crisply, leading the way slowly up the stairs, and along the passage towards Zarco's wing of the house.

'This isn't the right room!' Tiffany protested, as Amy took hold of her arm and steered her firmly into the large bedroom, whose rich jewel colours gleamed in the midday sun.

'It's the Marquês's orders. It's more than my life is worth not to do as he says!' Amy retorted, her cheeks reddening slightly as Tiffany gazed at her in astonishment. 'And not before time too, if you ask me!' the older woman muttered under her breath as she bustled off to run a bath for the clearly exhausted girl, who looked as if she was going to collapse at any minute.

'What is—er—the Marquês doing in Amsterdam?' Tiffany asked, when she was being helped into the comfortable bed by Amy.

After a swift look at the girl as she lay listlessly back against the pillows, Amy hesitated for a moment. 'I expect he'll tell you all about it when he gets home tomorrow,' she murmured, before drawing the cur-

tains and advising Tiffany to try and have a good
sleep.

And, despite her conviction that 'a good sleep' was
quite beyond her, Tiffany realised that she must have
drifted off, because it was many hours later when she
opened her eyes—to find herself blinking dazedly up
at the tall, commanding figure of Zarco.

Still not fully awake, she gazed sleepily at the man
standing beside the bed; the arrogant Brazilian, who
had totally dominated her life for the past month or
so.

Dressed in a dark formal suit, his black tie starkly
etched against the crisp white silk shirt, he looked
particularly formidable. And yet, beneath the surface
of his tanned complexion, his skin looked grey, with
deep lines of strain etched on either side of his mouth
and dark shadows beneath his eyes, which gave his
handsome features a drawn, haggard appearance.

'How are you feeling?' he asked quietly.

She couldn't answer him immediately. Her heart was
too overflowing with love and tenderness to be able
to find the words to answer his polite enquiry.

'I'm much better,' she managed at last, careful to
avoid his eyes as he helped her to sit up, holding the
glass of water as she took a small sip. 'Did . . . did you
have a good trip?'

'No, I didn't.' He frowned, as if her question was
an unnecessary irrelevance, before grating, 'I hope
Amy has been looking after you properly?'

'Yes, she's been very kind,' Tiffany whispered,
staring down at her nervously twisting hands, and
swallowing hard to keep her tears at bay. 'I don't mean
to be a nuisance. I promise you that I'll leave—just
as soon as I'm fit and well. I may have to borrow

some money, of course, but I'm sure that I can soon find a job...' she babbled, suddenly frightened of this tall, seemingly remote-looking stranger, who was now gazing down at her with barely concealed anger in his glittering eyes.

'That's *all* I need!' he exploded furiously. 'Don't you realise just how much agony you've caused me? You were only unconscious for a day—but, I swear to God, it must have been quite the longest, most terrifying twenty-four hours of my life!'

She cringed back against the pillows as his rage seemed to fill the large room.

'I didn't mean ... it really was an accident!' she exclaimed helplessly. 'I was only trying to get away from the awful man, Tony. He seemed convinced that I knew where "the loot" was hidden. And he also seemed totally convinced that I was Maxine! I was so frightened ... I couldn't think what to do ... and then I saw you, and ...'

'Hush, my darling!' he murmured, swiftly casting aside his anger and fury as he sat down on the bed, gathering her shaking, trembling figure into his arms. 'It's all over now. You're quite safe, and there's nothing more to worry about,' he murmured soothingly.

Just my broken heart—that's all, she told herself miserably, unable to prevent herself from savouring the warmth and security of his strong embrace. It was wrong for her to be leaning weakly against his broad shoulders like this—and she'd never do it again, of course. But surely she would be forgiven for seeking the sanctuary of his arms ... just this once?

'Please don't be cross with me,' she whispered tearfully against the soft cashmere of his suit jacket. 'I know it was an idiotic thing to do—to run into a van, but——'

'*Deus*, Tiffany—are you mad? I'm not cross with *you*!' he exclaimed incredulously, his hands holding her away from him for a moment as he studied her pale face, and the tears welling up in her sapphire-blue eyes. 'It was the hideous danger you were in that I found so terrifying. When I saw you lying on the drive, like a limp rag doll,' he growled, his voice hoarse and grating, 'I nearly went berserk! I was convinced that you were dead, and I was almost out of my mind with shock. And, even when the doctors said you would live, I was so frightened that you would remain forever in a deep coma; that I would lose you— my heart's desire—forever!'

She had grown pale at the suppressed force behind his huskily voiced words, unable to believe what she was hearing.

'But Zarco, I don't understand . . .' she breathed, before he clasped her tightly in his arms once more, his lips possessing hers with a great hunger that said far more than mere words could possibly have conveyed.

Her slim arms wound themselves about his neck and she melted beneath the heat of his scorching kiss— desperately craving the touch of his lips on hers; a need and a desire so intense that she could almost die for it. And she couldn't bear for him to stop, because when he did she knew that she would have to be brave; to find some courage from goodness knows where, and force herself to bid a final, agonising farewell to the only man she had ever loved.

When Zarco reluctantly let her go some moments later, it was all she could do to open her eyes and look at him.

'The doctors tell me that I must take good care of you,' he said huskily, settling her carefully back against the pillows. 'Although, only the good lord knows how I am to keep my hands away from your delicious body!'

She shuddered at the sensual words, the hoarse note in his voice sending shivers feathering up and down her spine.

'Zarco—we really must be sensible!' she gasped, her own voice tremulous as she tried to find the right words which would finally put an end to their relationship.

'*Sensible* . . . ?' He gazed at her with incredulity, before giving a short bark of laughter. 'I never cease to be astonished by the English—or their use of the language! How can I possibly be *sensible* at such a time?' he added scathingly. 'I come from a Latin race—so kindly do not speak to me of sense and sensibility, when all *I* wish to talk about is my love for you!'

'But . . . but you can't!'

'No? And who is to tell me what I can and cannot do?' he demanded, with a return of his old arrogance.

'No—you misunderstood me. What I meant . . . what I was trying to say——' But she wasn't given a chance to finish the sentence, as Zarco leaned forward and kissed her.

This was madness! She *must* stop him! she told herself desperately. But the tender touch of his warm lips, and the moist excitement of his probing tongue as his kiss deepened, completely swept away all rational thought.

'I love you,' his murmured, his voice thick with a yearning hunger as he reluctantly raised his dark head. 'I love you, my dearest Tiffany, with all my heart!'

'And I love *you*!' she cried tearfully, caught up in a white-hot, feverish turmoil of thwarted desire and passion. 'But there's Maxine! We can't just behave as if she didn't exist, can we?'

If she had hoped that her words would bring him to his senses, it seemed that she had succeeded only too well. For one moment he stared at her with shocked, horrified eyes, and then sighed as he slowly rose to his feet.

'You cannot know, of course,' he said, as much to himself as to her, before walking slowly over to stare out of the window, which was open to the soft night air.

'Know what?' She gazed at his tall figure in bewilderment.

He didn't reply for a moment, continuing to stare blindly out of the window. 'I was not able to be with you when you were in the hospital in London,' he said at last. 'For the very good reason that I received a sudden call from Amsterdam to say that my wife had been killed in a car crash. It was a head-on collision with another vehicle, while she was being chased by the Dutch police. Luckily, the occupants of the other car escaped with their lives.'

Tiffany stared at him in horror. 'What ... what was Maxine doing in Amsterdam?'

'It is the centre of the diamond trade, and it seems she was trying to sell my family's jewellery,' Zarco said, before giving a heavy sigh and pushing a tired hand through his dark hair. 'My agents had managed to track her down, at long last, and alerted the police. They were waiting for her in the shop, but she must have smelled a rat. Leaving the diamonds and emeralds behind her, she apparently ran out of the shop, jumped into a nearby car that had been foolishly parked with its keys still in the ignition, and must have been so intent on evading the police that she didn't look where she was going.' He gave a sad, weary shake of his head and sighed heavily once again.

'I think I should tell you that I've remembered what happened to me in Portugal. When I woke up in hospital, it was all there in my mind,' Tiffany said quietly, before giving him a brief outline of what had happened to her, following her meeting with his wife in the health club in Lisbon.

'Yes... Maxine was truly an evil woman—and what she did to you was unforgivable,' he said sorrowfully as he began to slowly remove his jacket. 'It all seems such a waste, somehow. Maxine was born with so many gifts: beauty, brains, courage... but they were all turned to corruption and wickedness by a twisted, vicious streak in her basic character.'

'What happens now?' Tiffany asked hesitantly. 'Do you have to go back to Amsterdam?'

He shook his head. 'No. The funeral was yesterday,' he said, taking off his black tie. 'It was a bit of an ordeal, breaking the news to her father over the phone. He took it very well, but I hadn't the heart to tell him about Tony Silver.'

'That awful man!' She shuddered. 'He was involved in the theft with Maxine, you know.'

'He was involved in far more than that!' Zarco told her grimly. 'While you and I have been going through the torments of hell, and agonising about my so-called "adultery", the agents I employed to dig up the details of Maxine's past have now come up with a pretty kettle of fish. It seems, my dear Tiffany, that I was never *legally* Maxine's husband...because she'd never obtained a divorce from her first husband, Antonio Salvatore—alias Tony Silver!'

'*What*?'

Zarco gave a short bark of rueful laughter. 'I really *was* a fool, wasn't I? I never thought to check out her background. But, if I had, I would have discovered that Tony Silver had fallen foul of the mob, in New York. Fearing for his life, he apparently arranged his fake death, and then escaped to Europe to lie low for a bit. In the meantime, Maxine—who had obviously been involved in Tony's arrangements—played the grieving widow to perfection. And her so-called marriage to me convinced Tony's bosses that he was indeed dead.'

'I can hardly believe this! You mean to say...?'

'Yes. Maxine's marriage to me was totally illegal. She was still Tony's wife—right up to the day she died. It's incredible, no?'

Tiffany stared at him with dazed eyes. 'So why did Tony turn up here, of all places?'

Zarco shrugged. 'It seems that Maxine had tried to double-cross him over the jewellery. Although I'm not totally certain about this, it appears that the original plan was for them both to carry out the theft, before disappearing together. But then...Maxine met you, my darling, and had a *much* better idea. If she could convince everyone that she had been killed, they wouldn't have been looking for her, would they? And with *all* the money from the sale of the jewels she could live very well for a number of years, with no fear that I would be trying to track her down.'

'But that's crazy!' Tiffany shook her head in helpless bewilderment. 'Ordinary people simply don't do that sort of thing!'

'You're quite right. But then, Maxine wasn't an ordinary person. And her plan wasn't so crazy—because it very nearly worked,' Zarco added, a note of grim savagery in his voice. 'If a stranger hadn't seen you struggling with Maxine and Tony on top of the cliff, and raised the alarm, this story would have had quite a different ending!'

'I simply can't seem to take all this in,' Tiffany muttered, her head spinning with confusion.

'I still find the whole business quite extra-ordinary—and I've had some days to absorb all the facts,' he agreed, coming over to sit down beside her, and gently brushing a small lock of hair from her brow.

'And you were *never* really married to Maxine?'

'No. I'm afraid that I have been made to look a complete fool.' He gave a rueful shake of his dark head.

'But... but I still don't understand why she went to all those lengths, and...'

'Two million pounds is a great deal of money,' Zarco told her quietly. 'And, since there was obviously a risk that divorcing me would have brought her dubious past to light, Maxine clearly decided to settle for what she could steal from my safety deposit box instead.'

'But why involve me?'

He sighed. 'My darling, I realise that you must have so many questions. But it has been a long day. So I'm going to have a shower, and then we'll ask Amy to serve us a meal, and then...' He leaned forward to give her a soft kiss on her forehead. 'Then we must make arrangements for a wedding. I am hoping that you will take pity on me—and make sure that I am *legally* married to someone, at long last!'

Tiffany gasped. 'You mean...?'

'I will leave you to work it out,' he grinned, giving her another swift kiss before rising from the bed and disappearing into his bathroom.

CHAPTER NINE

WHEN Zarco returned from having a shower, Tiffany, whose brain was still whirling in dazed confusion, could only stare helplessly at the man whom she loved with all her heart.

Wearing only a short white towel about the slim waist of his tall, lean body, his tanned skin still bearing tiny droplets of water from the shower, he looked impossibly handsome. Zarco *must* be every woman's dream hero, she told herself unhappily—quite unable to believe that he truly loved her.

'How is your poor head?' he murmured, coming over to sit down on the bed beside her.

In far better shape than my poor heart, she thought wildly, unable to tear her eyes away from the strong muscles of his bronze torso.

'There's nothing really wrong with me,' she told him huskily. 'The hospital were just worried because it was my second bout of unconsciousness.'

'Ah, yes.' He shook his dark head, sighing heavily as he clasped hold of her nervously trembling hands. 'They were quite right to be concerned. When I arrived at the hospital in Lisbon, I was warned that you might not survive your accident. You appeared to be in such a deep coma that I feared the worst.'

'But...but that was still when you thought that I was Maxine, so...'

'I cannot pretend that I felt anything for her, other than considerable repugnance and dislike,' Zarco said slowly. 'But I can promise you that I *never* wished her any physical harm—certainly not her recent and most shocking death. I hope you will believe what I say?' he added, looking at her with concern.

'Yes, of course I believe you,' she reassured him quickly. 'I can remember asking why you hadn't bumped her off years ago—and being surprised at just how forcefully you rejected the very idea of doing such a thing.'

He shook his head sorrowfully. 'I was not kind to you in Lisbon.'

'No—you certainly were not!' She gave a shaky laugh. 'I was simply *terrified* when I first saw you.' She shuddered. 'Not only did I think that you were the devil incarnate, but, quite honestly, I don't think I've *ever* been so frightened in all my life as when I woke up to find you looming menacingly over my bed!'

'But you must try to understand the situation in which I found myself,' he said quickly. 'I was very tired and full of jet lag after a long plane journey. And there was my wife—who had been no wife to me—lying unconscious in hospital. I could not understand why she was in Lisbon, or what she was doing there. Although, knowing her as I did, I knew that some trickery must lie behind her unexpected visit to that city. And yet...' He sighed deeply.

'I became desperately confused by your obvious fear of me, and of your sweet gentleness—both responses so completely unlike those of Maxine. And I must also confess...' He paused, his cheeks reddening slightly. 'I was also *very* confused and upset to find myself feeling a strong sexual urge and attraction towards a woman whom I disliked; a woman I had never touched since the day of our marriage.'

'Oh, Zarco—what a mess it all was!' Tiffany sighed.

He gave a low, rueful bark of laughter. 'That, my darling, is a complete understatement! The situation became even more complicated when I discovered the theft from my safety deposit box. I was *so* angry and furious—not so much at the loss of the gold and valuable jewellery as at myself for having been careless enough to let Maxine get away with such a plan—that I couldn't see beyond the end of my nose. If I am to be honest, I must confess that it was my pride that was hurt most of all,' he added with a wry grimace. 'And, of course, I now realise that I had already begun to fall in love with you. So I'm afraid that my frustrated desire only added more fuel to the flames of my ever increasing rage and fury.'

'You always seemed to be in a blind rage with me,' she agreed sadly. 'But surely you must have known fairly soon—or at least suspected—that I wasn't Maxine?'

'Yes, I think I did,' he muttered, letting go of her hands to brush his fingers agitatedly through his damp hair. 'But my emotions were in such a turmoil that for some time I simply didn't know *what* to think. At one point, I seriously feared that I was losing my sanity. Especially since I could hardly manage to keep my hands off you . . . !' he breathed, leaning forward to give her a long, ardent kiss.

'Don't!' she begged as his lips left hers to press butterfly-soft kisses over the soft contours of her face.

'Don't—what?' he murmured, trailing his warm mouth down the long line of her throat.

'We shouldn't be doing this. I've only just come out of hospital, for heaven's sake!' she gasped, her voice barely audible as he pressed his moist lips to the swell of her breasts, rising above the bodice of her thin silk nightgown.

'Then you must just lie still—and do as you're told!' he teased gently as he slipped the thin straps of the gown from her shoulders, exposing her full breasts to his view.

The feel of his long tanned fingers on her burgeoning flesh seemed to trigger an instinctive response quite beyond her control. Gazing mistily down at his dark head as he caressed her breasts, tracing the outline of her nipples with his tongue, before drawing the hard peaks into his mouth, she couldn't help gasping with delight, a helpless victim of the sweet, urgent ache which seemed to possess her whole body.

Lost in a sweeping blur of overriding passion, she trembled beneath the waves of desire and longing crashing over her as he gently and carefully removed her gown, before he slowly and tantalisingly began to kiss his way down her slim figure. His lips seemed to be on fire, branding her flesh with the mark of his fervent possession and love as he sought and found every secret part of her body.

'*Zarco*!' she cried, writhing with ecstasy as he pressed his mouth to the heated centre of her flesh, the mounting excitement causing small helpless moans to break from the back of her throat as she shuddered convulsively beneath the erotic, sensual rasp of his tongue. And then he urgently tossed away the small towel he'd been wearing, and as his strong body covered hers she felt the hot, velvety thrust of his strong thighs.

'I love you, my sweet Tiffany,' he breathed thickly. 'I will always love and worship you ... for the rest of my life.'

The sound of his husky vow seemed to fill her ears as the world faded away, leaving only their two bodies moving together in a delicious, exciting rhythm that was as old as time itself, before spiralling headlong into a whirling vortex of rapturous joy and total commitment.

Much later, as Tiffany lay drowsily cradled in his arms, he murmured, 'I know it was not wise to make love to you—not when you have yet to recover from your injuries. But, my sweet one, I *really* couldn't help myself! I was selfishly possessed of an overwhelming need and desire to demonstrate my total love for you,' he added with a sigh.

'Oh, Zarco...' she whispered, almost unable to believe her own happiness. 'Are you sure? Are you *quite* sure that you and I ... that we...?'

'I am certain that I love you,' he said firmly, the hard conviction in his voice allaying her numerous fears. 'I am also totally determined to make you my wife—as soon as possible. We will have a quiet wedding, here in the village church, and then I will take you away with me on the Orient Express to stay at the Cipriani Hotel in Venice.'

'Are you *always* going to make all the important decisions in our life?' she asked with a slight frown.

'Of course! Do you *seriously* believe that I am likely to change my character?' he grinned, softly kissing away the small crease from her brow.

'No, I'm afraid I don't!' she laughed. 'But why Venice?'

He gave a slight shrug of his powerful shoulders. 'Because you have never been there, and I am quite sure that you will be entranced by that lovely city. And also,' he added, the warm smile dying from his face, 'I don't wish to start my married life with you in Brazil, which holds far too many memories for me. And we will be spending much of our future life both here in England and on my large estate, in the south of Portugal. So... Venice seems a good choice, hmm?'

'Yes... it sounds marvellous,' she agreed, wondering how to frame her next and very important question. 'I—er—I've never talked to you about your first wife, Zarco. I don't want... I mean, I know you loved her very deeply, and...'

'That was a long time ago,' he said firmly. 'I was a much younger and quite different man when I was married to Charlotte. And, although I have grieved most sincerely for the tragic loss of her young life, she is now a warm and much loved memory in my heart. What I feel for you, Tiffany, is a totally different emotion. It is not that of the young, callow youth that I once was. It is a mature and adult passion; a desire not just for your body, lovely though it is, but for the kindness and sweetly caring nature of your soul.'

'Oh, *Zarco*!' she whispered, quite overcome by his words, and her total happiness in being in his arms. 'I will try to be a good stepmother to Charlie,' she promised.

'I have absolutely no doubt that you will succeed. The boy is clearly already very fond of you, and I'm sure that he will be thrilled to have some new sisters to play with.'

She gazed up at him in bewilderment. 'Sisters . . . ?'

'I would like some lovely daughters—just like their mother!' He smiled down into her dazed eyes.

'Oh—goodness! I hadn't thought about having a baby. I mean, everything has happened so fast, and...'

'You might even be carrying my child at this moment,' he murmured, placing a possessive hand on the bare flesh of her flat stomach.

'Well, I would like a little time for just the two of us—and Charlie as well, of course,' she told him firmly. 'I think you're going to be quite enough to deal with, before I have to cope with any more of the dos Santos family!'

'You will manage us all perfectly,' he told her with a slow smile, his fingers beginning to move sensually over her body.

'No, really Zarco—not again! You can't . . . !' she gasped as his touch became more urgent and determined.

'Are you seriously suggesting that I cannot be permitted to make love to my future wife?' he demanded imperiously.

'Who—me? I wouldn't *dream* of even mentioning such heresy!' she giggled, before happily surrendering to the overwhelming force of her love for that hard, arrogant man—Zarco dos Santos.

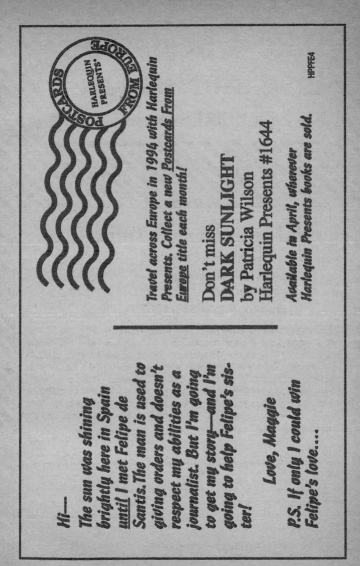

POSTCARDS FROM EUROPE

HARLEQUIN PRESENTS®

Travel across Europe in 1994 with Harlequin Presents. Collect a new <u>Postcards From Europe</u> title each month!

Don't miss
DARK SUNLIGHT
by Patricia Wilson
Harlequin Presents #1644

Available in April, wherever Harlequin Presents books are sold.

HPPFE4

Hi—
The sun was shining brightly here in Spain <u>until</u> I met Felipe de Santis. The man is used to giving orders and doesn't respect my abilities as a journalist. But I'm going to get my story—and I'm going to help Felipe's sister!

Love, Maggie

P.S. If only I could win Felipe's love....

Take 4 bestselling love stories FREE

Plus get a FREE surprise gift!

Special Limited-time Offer

Mail to Harlequin Reader Service®

3010 Walden Avenue
P.O. Box 1867
Buffalo, N.Y. 14269-1867

YES! Please send me 4 free Harlequin Presents® novels and my free surprise gift. Then send me 6 brand-new novels every month, which I will receive months before they appear in bookstores. Bill me at the low price of $2.44 each plus 25¢ delivery and applicable sales tax, if any*. That's the complete price and—compared to the cover prices of $2.99 each—quite a bargain! I understand that accepting the books and gift places me under no obligation ever to buy any books. I can always return a shipment and cancel at any time. Even if I never buy another book from Harlequin, the 4 free books and the surprise gift are mine to keep forever.

106 BPA ANRH

Name _____ (PLEASE PRINT) _____

Address _____ Apt. No. _____

City _____ State _____ Zip _____

This offer is limited to one order per household and not valid to present Harlequin Presents® subscribers. *Terms and prices are subject to change without notice. Sales tax applicable in N.Y.

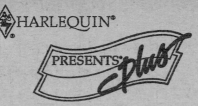

When the only time you have for yourself is...

STOLEN moments

Spring into spring—by giving yourself a March Break! Take a few *stolen moments* and treat yourself to a Great Escape. Relax with one of our brand-new stories (or with all six!).

Each STOLEN MOMENTS title in our Great Escapes collection is a complete and never-before-published *short* novel. These contemporary romances are 96 pages long—the perfect length for the busy woman of the nineties!

Look for Great Escapes in our Stolen Moments display this March!

SIZZLE by Jennifer Crusie
ANNIVERSARY WALTZ
by Anne Marie Duquette
MAGGIE AND HER COLONEL
by Merline Lovelace
PRAIRIE SUMMER by Alina Roberts
THE SUGAR CUP by Annie Sims
LOVE ME NOT by Barbara Stewart

Wherever Harlequin and Silhouette books are sold.

HARLEQUIN®

COMING SOON TO
A STORE NEAR YOU...

THE MAIN
ATTRACTION

By *New York Times* Bestselling Author

This March, look for THE MAIN ATTRACTION by popular
author Jayne Ann Krentz.

Ten years ago, Filomena Cromwell had left her small town
in shame. Now she is back determined to get her sweet,
sweet revenge....

Soon she has her ex-fiancé, who cheated on her with
another woman, chasing her all over town. And he isn't
the only one. Filomena lets Trent Ravinder catch her.

Can she control the fireworks she's set into motion?

HARLEQUIN®

Don't miss these Harlequin favorites by some of our most distin-
guished authors!
And now, you can receive a discount by ordering two or more titles!

HT#25409	THE NIGHT IN SHINING ARMOR by JoAnn Ross	$2.99	☐
HT#25471	LOVESTORM by JoAnn Ross	$2.99	☐
HP#11463	THE WEDDING by Emma Darcy	$2.89	☐
HP#11592	THE LAST GRAND PASSION by Emma Darcy	$2.99	☐
HR#03188	DOUBLY DELICIOUS by Emma Goldrick	$2.89	☐
HR#03248	SAFE IN MY HEART by Leigh Michaels	$2.89	☐
HS#70464	CHILDREN OF THE HEART by Sally Garrett	$3.25	☐
HS#70524	STRING OF MIRACLES by Sally Garrett	$3.39	☐
HS#70500	THE SILENCE OF MIDNIGHT by Karen Young	$3.39	☐
HI#22178	SCHOOL FOR SPIES by Vickie York	$2.79	☐
HI#22212	DANGEROUS VINTAGE by Laura Pender	$2.89	☐
HI#22219	TORCH JOB by Patricia Rosemoor	$2.89	☐
HAR#16459	MACKENZIE'S BABY by Anne McAllister	$3.39	☐
HAR#16466	A COWBOY FOR CHRISTMAS by Anne McAllister	$3.39	☐
HAR#16462	THE PIRATE AND HIS LADY by Margaret St. George	$3.39	☐
HAR#16477	THE LAST REAL MAN by Rebecca Flanders	$3.39	☐
HH#28704	A CORNER OF HEAVEN by Theresa Michaels	$3.99	☐
HH#28707	LIGHT ON THE MOUNTAIN by Maura Seger	$3.99	☐

Harlequin Promotional Titles

#83247	YESTERDAY COMES TOMORROW by Rebecca Flanders	$4.99	☐
#83257	MY VALENTINE 1993	$4.99	☐
	(short-story collection featuring Anne Stuart, Judith Arnold,
Anne McAllister, Linda Randall Wisdom)		

(limited quantities available on certain titles)

	AMOUNT	$
DEDUCT:	10% DISCOUNT FOR 2+ BOOKS	$
ADD:	POSTAGE & HANDLING	$
	($1.00 for one book, 50¢ for each additional)	
	APPLICABLE TAXES*	$ _____
	TOTAL PAYABLE	$ _____
	(check or money order—please do not send cash)	

To order, complete this form and send it, along with a check or money order for the
total above, payable to Harlequin Books, to: **In the U.S.:** 3010 Walden Avenue,
P.O. Box 9047, Buffalo, NY 14269-9047; **In Canada:** P.O. Box 613, Fort Erie, Ontario,
L2A 5X3.

Name: _____

Address: _____ City: _____

State/Prov.: _____ Zip/Postal Code: _____

*New York residents remit applicable sales taxes.
 Canadian residents remit applicable GST and provincial taxes.

HBACK-JM